THE BOLDS

by Julian Clary

Illustrated by David Roberts

Carolrhoda Books · Minneapolis

First published in 2015 by Andersen Press Limited
First American edition published in 2016 by Carolrhoda Books
Published by arrangement with Andersen Press Limited

Carolrhoda Books
A division of Lerner Publishing Group, Inc.
241 First Avenue North
Minneapolis, MN 55401 USA

For reading levels and more information,
look up this title at www.lernerbooks.com.

Main body text set in Century Schoolbook Std regular 12.5/21.
Typeface provided by Monotype Typography.

Library of Congress Cataloging-in-Publication Data

Clary, Julian, author.
    The Bolds / by Julian Clary ; illustrated by David Roberts.
       pages cm
    Summary: Two hyenas from Africa find a pair of passports (memo: do not go
 swimming in a crocodile pool), and move to Teddington, England, where they
 live suburban lives, hold jobs, and raise their children to hide their tails and
 act human—the only trouble is old Mr. McNumpty, their nosy neighbor, who is
 hiding a secret of his own.
    ISBN 978-1-5124-0440-1 (lb : alk. paper) — ISBN 978-1-5124-0443-2 (eb pdf)
    1. Hyenas—Juvenile fiction. 2. Neighbors—Juvenile fiction.
3. Impersonation—Juvenile fiction. 4. Secrecy—Juvenile fiction. 5. Humorous
stories. 6. Teddington (London, England)—Juvenile fiction. [1. Hyenas—Fiction.
2. Neighbors—Fiction. 3. Impersonation—Fiction. 4. Secrets—Fiction. 5.
Humorous stories. 6. Teddington (London, England)—Fiction. 7. England—
Fiction.] I. Roberts, David, 1970– illustrator. II. Title.
PZ7.1.C59Bo 2015
823.92—dc23
[Fic]   2015020875

Manufactured in the United States of America
2-43116-21105-5/4/2017

For my great nephews and nieces
Nico, Jake, Dani, Mia, Alex, and Zac

JC

Chapter

Telling lies is NEVER a good idea. I once told my friends that I was a sausage roll. I really, definitely was, I said. When they finally believed me, they **squirted me** with tomato ketchup and bit me on the leg.

"Stop it!" I had to shout in the end. "I'm not a sausage roll—I am a *human being!*"

That taught me a lesson, I can tell you. I don't tell lies any more. Ever.

So believe me when I say that the story I am going to tell you is ABSOLUTELY TRUE. It's important that you know and understand this, because it is quite an extraordinary story. And funny. Funny peculiar. Very funny peculiar, in fact.

But true. Every word.

The first thing you need to understand before I begin this story is that for some reason human beings have grown rather full of themselves over the years. They now believe that they are far cleverer than all other living creatures.

This is a mistake. Just because humans can read and write and use knives and forks and computers, they think they are better than other animals? How stupid! Did you know that a squirrel can hide ten thousand nuts in the woods and remember where every single one of them is hidden? Well, I ask you: could you remember where you'd put ten thousand nuts?

Frogs can sleep with their eyes open. Can you?

A cat can lick its own bottom! How clever is that?

The truth is that animals are just as clever as people, but clever in different ways. Animals think people are the stupid ones sometimes.

Next time you pass a field of sheep, stop and look: they will stare back at you with a steady, sympathetic gaze. If you look closely, though, you might see them shake their heads—amused that we need to wear sweaters and coats made out of wool that grows perfectly naturally on their backs. What a silly business!

But anyway, back to my story. It begins ten years ago, far away in Africa. Africa, as you may know from photographs and television programs, is a very hot and beautiful place. There are forests and bush and vast open plains where lots of wild animals live—lions and elephants and giraffes. There are brightly colored birds that live in the trees, monkeys and gorillas, lizards, hyenas, porcupines and buffaloes. The place is teeming with life of every size and shape you can imagine.

And in Africa, let me tell you, the wild animals are also very clever. They watch human beings and chuckle to themselves. "Fancy going around cooped up in air-conditioned buses and cars and eating boring cooked food! Humans all look so uncomfortable!

"We so-called 'wild' animals wander around freely," they say to each other. "Breathing the fresh air and eating fresh food that we catch or pick or graze for ourselves. Far better, in our humble opinion!"

Which lifestyle seems nicer to you?

All the animals in Africa know that the cleverest among them are the hyenas. They aren't the fastest or fiercest, or—let's face it—the most beautiful, but they are smart and determined and work together to get what they want. They are very good at scavenging too.

But the thing hyenas do best, and

which drives all the other animals crazy, is: they laugh.

In fact, they're known as laughing hyenas. Long, loud shrieks and cackles.

They
can outsmart
a pride of lions by
running circles around
them, laughing and snorting,
and then steal their dinner
in the confusion.

To be honest with you, hyenas are not very popular among the other animals. Birds sing prettily, lions roar impressively, but the incessant laughter of the clever hyenas gives the other animals a headache.

Now then. There was once a large clan of hyenas living in the Masai Mara (which is a huge national park in Africa). And these particular hyenas laughed even more than most.

They lived in burrows near to a safari camp, where lots of tourists came to see the animals in their natural environment. Slowly these hyenas became accustomed to their strange visitors. They would creep ever closer to the camp, scavenging leftover food, getting bolder and bolder. Eventually, over time, they began to understand the human way of communicating— they learned to understand human languages.

There were a lot of English visitors at this particular safari camp, so after a while the hyenas began to copy their language and they started to talk. In fact, their first words to each other in English were:

> Cucumber sandwich, anyone?

One day, a honeymoon couple at the safari camp foolishly wandered into the bush alone with nothing but their backpacks for protection. Finding the African midday sun too hot for them, they slipped out of their

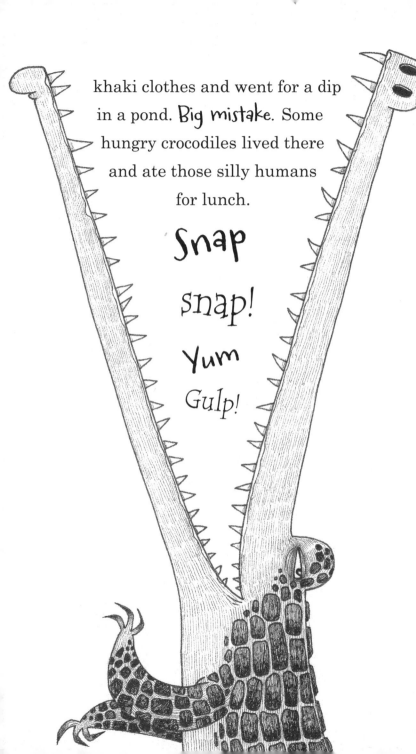

khaki clothes and went for a dip in a pond. **Big mistake**. Some hungry crocodiles lived there and ate those silly humans for lunch.

Snap

snap!

Yum

Gulp!

Two of the English-speaking hyenas, called Spot and Sue, who were actually very much in love, saw what had happened and came to sniff around the couple's discarded items.

"Hey!" said Spot to Sue. "Come and look at this!" And he handed her two passports, pulled from one of the bags.

"Well, well!" exclaimed Sue. "The poor dears were called Fred and Amelia Bold. May they rest in peace." The two hyenas stopped for a moment and bowed their heads as they thought about the poor dead humans.

But hyenas are known to be opportunistic creatures, and sure enough, Sue soon had a very daring idea.

"Can you walk on your hind legs, dear?" she asked Spot.

12

"Then listen," Sue said excitedly. "These clothes look like they might fit us. We could put them on and go back to the safari camp as Fred and Amelia Bold!"

"Then what?" asked Spot, frowning.

"Don't you see?" said Sue. "This is our way out of here. I've always fancied living in England. Apparently it isn't as hot as Africa and the humans there love lining up. That would make a nice change from always fighting and diving in for scraps of meat here with the rest of the hyena clan. This is our chance for a new life!"

"Oh my!" said Spot with an incredulous laugh. "That is one BOLD idea! Do you really think we could get away with it?"

"Why not?" said Sue as she continued to look through the dead couple's belongings.

"Look, here are two plane tickets, drivers licenses, house keys, car keys—and our new address: 41 Fairfield Road, Teddington,in Middlesex, England . . ."

"It does have a nice ring to it," said Spot, as he slipped into the large pair of shorts. "And I must say, these are a perfect fit."

"Tuck your tail out of the way, for goodness' sake! It's peeking out the bottom of your shorts. That would give the game away."

Spot laughed. "Oh, Sue, how I love you!" he said, trying on a green sun hat.

"I'm not Sue any more, remember?" she replied, putting on a fancy voice as she buttoned up her khaki shirt. "From now on, you must call me Amelia. And you, my husband, are Fred! We are Fred and Amelia Bold."

And with that they both rolled around laughing, before they got up on their hind legs to walk back to the camp and into a new life.

Chapter

I did warn you it was a very unusual story, didn't I? Good. So, dressed in human clothes and walking on their hind legs, the two hyenas slipped into England and began their new life as Fred and Amelia Bold.

It wasn't easy. Their tails had to be kept hidden at all times. As a rule, people don't have tails, and there was likely to be talk if the Bolds were spotted swishing them about all over the place.

They also discovered they looked far more human-like if they wore hats (as well as clothes). Spot (now Fred) wore the green hat he had found among Fred's things, and Sue (now Amelia) made herself a very fetching turban out of Amelia's scarves—which covered her large ears wonderfully.

They also realized very quickly that humans don't laugh nearly as much as hyenas, and it didn't do to draw attention to themselves. In fact, a flight attendant had gotten angry with them on the plane to England for laughing too much when she did her flight safety demonstration.

They had to learn to bottle up their laughter until they were safely home, and even then they sometimes had to cover their snouts with a pillow in case the neighbors became suspicious.

"We mustn't draw attention to ourselves, dear," said Fred. "People stare enough as it is."

It is true to say that people in Teddington considered them to be an unusual couple. But no one jumped to the conclusion that they were a pair of hyenas. And because they both laughed all day long, people decided they must be a fun couple to be around and they made friends easily.

Children were sometimes a bit harder to trick. But that's because children are often a lot cleverer and more observant than their parents. You've probably noticed that yourself.

You'll be on the bus and someone gets on who looks very different, or has something rather unusual about them, and as soon as you say, "Mum, why does that man . . . ?" all the adults around you immediately say, "Shush, it's rude to stare." And they never seem to notice that the people look different.

That's what happened to Amelia a few times in the early days. Children would stare at her and tug on their parents' sleeves. But they were quickly told not to point, and before long Amelia had learned that once she had glasses on and a colorful turban, not even children noticed her snout-like nose and pointy teeth.

The hyenas' new home at 41 Fairfield Road was very nice, they thought. A three-bedroom house with a pretty garden, and a garage with a shiny blue Honda parked inside.

"It makes our old burrow seem very dirty and dingy. Lovely to have windows to look out of!" said Amelia when they first arrived.

"I have a very strong urge to dig a hole in the garden," confessed Fred, biting his lip and pawing the air as if he were digging furiously there and then.

"So have I!" agreed Amelia. "But we'd better wait till it gets dark."

There was a lot they had to learn, and quickly. Crossing the road, for instance, was tricky at first—a bit like diving out the way of a charging rhino, they agreed.

And shopping was a strange business. It was only by watching how humans behaved that they realized you had to pay for everything.

"What a nuisance!"
said Amelia as they
wandered around
the supermarket.

"Yes," Fred sighed.
"It's called 'money,'
apparently. You keep
it in a purse and you
can't take the food
home until you've lined up
at the checkout and swapped it for bits of
paper and round pieces of metal."

"It's all completely bonkers!" said Amelia,
trying not to laugh too loudly.

But this money business was going to be a
problem, they realized. They had found some
bits of paper known as "cash" in a bedroom
drawer, but it wouldn't last forever.

"I've been reading in a magazine that people have things called 'jobs,'" announced Amelia one day.

"Isn't that when you go to the toilet?" asked Fred innocently. "Big jobs?"

"Ha ha ha heeee!" shrieked Amelia. "No! People go to work, in an office or somewhere. This is called their 'job.'"

"Why would they do that?"

"Well, then you get given money, kind of in exchange for your trouble, so you can buy food and clothes."

"Isn't it silly?!" said Fred when he finally understood.

"Well, yes it is," agreed Amelia as she picked up a pile of papers from the kitchen table. "But money will help pay these."

"What are they?" asked Fred.

"They're called bills."

"Bills? Like Bill and Bob?"

"Unfortunately not. You know the lovely fresh water we drink out of the tap?"

"Yes—delicious!" said Fred.

"Well," Amelia explained, "it isn't free. We have to pay for it."

"No!" Fred was confused. "But water falls from the sky! No one owns water, so how come it costs us money?"

Amelia shook her head. "Don't ask me. But here is a bill. And another for the nice warm radiators and the handy electric light. Everything but EVERYTHING costs MONEY!" She threw the pile of papers in the air. The bills fluttered silently down over the two thoughtful hyenas.

Eventually Fred spoke. "So . . . what are we going to do?"

Amelia smiled. "Don't worry. We will have to get jobs, that's all. Earn some money. What would you like to do? Or be?"

"A train driver!" answered Fred at once. "All aboard! Mind the gap! Vroom vroom! Mind the doors!"

When she had finished laughing, Amelia sighed. "No, dear. I don't think so."

"Taxi driver?" suggested Fred. He had learned to drive the little Honda on careful exploratory trips around Teddington Lock, but he wasn't very good at roundabouts.

"Er, maybe not," said Amelia, remembering the time Fred had driven straight across the middle of a roundabout instead of going round it. "You need to work at something you're good at."

There was a bit of a silence after that.

It wasn't easy, let's face it. Two unemployed

hyenas disguised as people . . . what on earth were they to do?

Weeks went by and the money from the drawer was soon gone. The pile of bills grew higher and higher. They got so hungry they had to slip into the park after dark and catch a few squirrels to eat. Fred even went down to the supermarket trash cans and came home with some out-of-date hamburger meat.

But eventually their luck changed. Amelia started selling her turbans at a stall at the local market, soon branching into unusual hats made of egg boxes, clothes pegs and old birds' nests, which became very popular

for Teddington ladies to wear at weddings. Fred too found the perfect job for him—writing the jokes that went inside Christmas crackers. He didn't have to be serious at all, and could laugh all day without anyone minding.

So Amelia and Fred became very happy living their new life. The weather wasn't as hot and stifling as in Africa. People looked sideways at them sometimes, but no one knew they were really hyenas. And they earned enough money to pay the bills and go shopping.

They thought they couldn't be happier, until one night, after what she thought was a bit of a stomachache brought on by a moldy burger, Amelia gave birth to twins—or should I say pups?

And the Bolds laughed and laughed with joy.

Chapter

The Bold children—a boy and a girl whom Fred and Amelia decided to call Bobby and Betty—were delightful bundles of furry fun.

Of course their parents loved them dearly, but as babies the two children did have a tendency to howl rather than cry, and it took a long time to teach them how to stand on their hind legs. But still, once they were in diapers, wearing baby clothes and floppy bonnets, no one really noticed any difference. And as Mr. Bold pushed them proudly through the park in their stroller, people would stop and say, "Don't they look like you!" and never finish by

saying, "And you look just like a wild animal," in the same way people don't say about ugly babies, "Oh, he looks just like a toad," even if they're thinking it.

The twins grew up to be happy and boisterous, full of fun and, of course, laughter.

They both had big, brown eyes and wide, smiling mouths with sharp, white teeth. Betty had darker wiry hair, which was tied in two small bunches just behind her cute— but rather large—round ears. Bobby's hair was blond and speckled, and stuck up in tufts on the top of his head.

Sometimes when they were playing, rolling around together wrestling, Betty would nip Bobby and he would yelp until Mrs. Bold picked him up and comforted him. But most of the time he was a cheerful little scamp who would tease his sister until she chased him round the house and into the garden.

Of course there came a time when Mr. and Mrs. Bold had to tell their children the truth about who they really were.

It was difficult for them. How on earth do you break it to a small child that they really aren't a child at all but a wild animal? A hyena, no less!

But Betty and Bobby had to be told before they started school, because of their tails— which needed to be hidden at all times, for obvious reasons. Trust me, a big hairy tail dangling behind you during a gym class would not go unnoticed in most schools!

"But they are such happy children," said Mrs. Bold sadly. "It seems a shame to give them something to worry about."

"Yes, dear, it does," agreed Mr. Bold. "But we must! It's all part of growing up and passing as a human being. Like learning to cross the road."

"And not blowing raspberries in public," said Mrs. Bold. "They can't seem to stop doing that."

So when the twins were old enough for school, their parents decided the moment had arrived. And that night, instead of a bedtime story, they announced they were going to have a serious talk with their children. Well, as serious as they could manage.

"We've got something to tell you," Mr. Bold began. "But it's a secret."

Mrs. Bold stifled an excited giggle.

"It's like this," Mr. Bold continued. "Have you ever noticed that we, as a family, are different from other people?"

"We've got more hair?" suggested Betty, stroking her furry arm.

"Yes, that's part of it," said her father.

"Other people get cross sometimes?" said Bobby. "We don't. We just laugh at everything, no matter what."

"Exactly!" said Mr. Bold.

"I don't know how to be cross," said Mrs. Bold. "The very idea of it just makes me shrieeek!" She began to laugh hysterically.

"Please, dear," said Mr. Bold. "Don't start me off."

"I'm sorry, darling. Do go on." She squeezed her long nose to stop the laughter.

"Yes. We must tell them. We really must."

"Tell us what?" asked Bobby.

"First of all, you must both promise that what I am about to tell you will remain a secret. You can never tell ANYONE. Do you understand?"

The children nodded solemnly.

And so their parents told them the whole, almost unbelievable story. They showed them pictures and videos of Africa and of all the wild animals, including hyenas. And they revealed the secret they'd kept hidden for many years.

"But listen, Betty and Bobby," said Mr. Bold, "no one, but NO ONE, must ever know we are not really human beings. Do you understand?" The twins could tell from their father's unusually stern tone of voice that he meant it. "Don't get me wrong—we are hyenas and we are proud of it—but if people found out, we'd be in trouble."

The children were shocked but then Mrs. Bold revealed another secret she'd discovered during her time in Teddington. At first she'd thought she was mistaken, but no, the more she looked around her, the more she was convinced that the Bolds were not the only animals living secretly as humans.

"We animals can spot a fellow animal, my dears," she told the children, "but humans have no idea. I don't think they'd like it if they knew just how many animals were pretending to be humans and living close by—"

"Oh no, they wouldn't," interrupted Mr. Bold. "There'd be a huge uproar if they ever found out."

"How many animals *are* there living as people?" asked Bobby.

"Oh, more than you would think," said Mrs. Bold. "You see, we've realized that animals have moved in as people all over the place. It's just that no one knows. I'm not one to tell tales, but there are a couple of giraffes living in Richmond. Shelf stockers at Waitrose . . . the perfect job for them." She paused to let this fact sink in.

Betty's eyes boggled. "You're sure?"

"Uh-huh," nodded her mother. "Have you ever noticed that some people look a little foxy? Or owlish? Or, ahem, hippopotamus like?

Well, that's because they are! Their true animal characteristics are there for all to see, but humans fail to put two and two together. If a footballer runs like a gazelle, then the chances are he is a gazelle. If someone eats like a pig . . . well, you get what I mean . . ." And she howled with laughter.

"Most important for us," said Mr. Bold, serious again, "and all the other 'secret' animals, are CLOTHES. Clothes allow us to hide the main thing that would give us away. Our TAILS!"

Clothes—pants, underwear, trousers, dresses, and coats—it was explained, were the Bolds' best friends. Tails waggled about when they were happy, and disappeared between their legs when they were nervous or unhappy (which, to be honest, wasn't very often). They had to learn to keep them hidden.

The pups seemed to take this new information in stride. Children are very adaptable, aren't they? With the help of some sturdy underwear and sticky tape, their tails were kept well concealed and they ran around charming everyone they met with their happy personalities.

Soon after this "serious" talk from their parents, the twins started at the local elementary school. Their slightly odd appearance was forgotten after a couple of days because they made everyone laugh.

Unfortunately, this also got them into all sorts of trouble.

"Where is your homework?" Mrs. Millin, the teacher, asked Bobby one day.

"The dog ate it," he replied.

"That is a very poor excuse!"

"Well, it's true. I had to smear it with dog food first, but he managed to get it down eventually."

The twins, although they were always

being scolded, made plenty of friends at school. They weren't naughty, but they were silly. And as the years went by, they got a lot noisier and were constantly whooping and chattering, shrieking and laughing.

Their best friend was a girl called Minnie, who lived above the butcher's shop in Teddington High Street, where her father, George, worked. Minnie was rather tall for her age and wanted to be a famous actress with a zillion Twitter followers when she grew up. She didn't like lessons much and didn't think she'd have much need for math or reading or writing when she was living in Hollywood, which meant she had plenty of time to mess around with the twins and get up to mischief. The twins and Minnie were *always* getting in trouble, usually for laughing during classes.

One day all three of them hooted so loudly during gym (when the twins climbed up a rope upside-down) that their punishment was to stay in the classroom during recess. Now, unfortunately, the twins' fangs had recently started to grow through, and that day they both felt an overwhelming urge to chew things, much to Minnie's amusement. So during that boring recess, when they should have been writing an essay about how wrong it

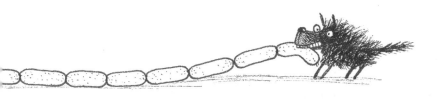

is to laugh during classes, they chomped their way through their pencils instead. Having got the taste for it they couldn't stop. After all, this would have been perfectly natural if they were hyenas growing up in Africa. It wasn't their fault that they were stuck in a school classroom in Teddington.

"How about chewing the chair legs next?" said Minnie encouragingly. She had gotten used to their funny ways over the years and

just thought they were hilarious. The twins were drooling with satisfaction.

"Delicious!" said Bobby, setting to work on the teacher's wooden chair.

"Tastes like pork scratchings!" agreed Betty, spluttering bits of splintered pine over the floor.

"You two are so funny!" said Minnie, holding her sides with laughter. After a few minutes of very enjoyable gnawing, the bell rang. Reluctantly the twins wiped their jaws clean and returned to their seats just in time, before the rest of the class returned and the next lesson began.

"Now then, children," said Mrs. Millin, as she sat herself down. "Who can spell the word—?" But before she could finish the sentence there was a loud creaking and her chair collapsed, crashing to the ground. Poor Mrs. Millin landed on her back, her big navy-blue knickers on show to all the children—who couldn't help but snigger. But it was the Bold twins who laughed loudest.

They were in big trouble once again.

Chapter

I haven't told you much about Teddington yet, have I? Well, it's a charming little place—I myself used to live there, many moons ago. There's a high street and a broad street, a station with trains taking people up to London, and a lovely big park—Bushy Park.

As for Fairfield Road, well, that's a pretty tree-lined street where the people like to keep themselves to themselves, which sounds perfect for our hyena family, doesn't it?

But unfortunately there was one exception to this rule—a bad-tempered, nosy old man called Mr. McNumpty. He had no friends, and he never smiled, and he had nothing nice to say about anyone. Particularly the Bolds. And just their luck, he lived right next door to them.

It was hard to tell how old he was—that's if he had ever been young. He had straggly white hair that poked out from under a silly fez hat, and a long, runny nose that he wiped on his sticky and stained sleeve. He had big, rounded shoulders and a lumbering walk, as if his legs were stiff and painful.

He would bang on the wall if the Bolds laughed too loudly, and throw garbage over the garden fence when he thought no one was watching.

"You live like animals!" he'd shouted gruffly once, when Betty and Bobby were having a lovely time rolling about in a muddy flowerbed on the morning of their seventh birthday. Little did he know . . .

He didn't like children and he didn't like laughter. If the Bolds passed him on the street he would refuse to answer when they called out a cheery "Good morning!" He just scowled and crossed the road.

"Poor Mr. McNumpty," said Mrs. Bold. "I can't imagine being so miserable and bad-tempered all the time. Perhaps I'll make him a cake. That will cheer him up."

But it didn't. When she knocked on his door with a delicious Victoria sponge cake for him, he slammed the door in her face.

"What a horrid thing to do!" said Mrs. Bold, back in her own kitchen.

"Well, maybe he'd rather have a pie?" said Mr. Bold helpfully as the children wolfed down the unwanted cake.

"Or cupcakes?" suggested Betty.

"If you ask me . . . he's a fruitcake!" said Bobby, and this made everyone laugh.

One sunny, summer day the twins and Minnie were playing in the garden and Mr. McNumpty was next door up a ladder, cleaning his windows. There was a danger he might empty his bucket of water over the noisy children, but they hoped not.

Minnie had invented a new game called "Red Carpets," where the girls pretended to be beautiful actresses arriving at the Oscars, and Bobby was the paparazzi taking their photos.

Bobby set up his tripod (which was really three bamboo sticks held together with some string) and made sure there was some film in his camera (a tin of sardines). The girls had rooted around in the garden shed to find their ball gowns, which they made out of picnic blankets tied together precariously with some old tinsel and garden twine.

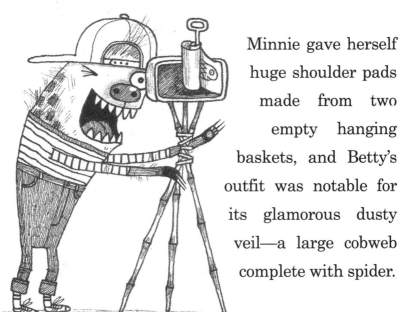

Minnie gave herself huge shoulder pads made from two empty hanging baskets, and Betty's outfit was notable for its glamorous dusty veil—a large cobweb complete with spider.

"This is what everyone is wearing in Paris this year," declared Minnie.

"Oh yes," said Betty. "And no one in Hollywood would dream of leaving home without a veil on these days."

"Hold it there, girls!" said Bobby, peering round the side of the sardine tin and raising one arm in the air. "Minnie, lower your chin a bit, please . . . Betty, it might make a better photo if you raised the veil a little so we can see some of your face. Lovely! Everyone say 'Smelly pants!' Beautiful!"

"Smelly pants!" said the girls.

Just then the spider on Betty's veil—none too thrilled at being moved into the sunshine from the shed—made a run for it and tickled the back of Betty's neck.

"What's that?" she cried, alarmed, and then sneezed loudly.

The tinsel that was holding her gown together suddenly fell apart and the blanket slipped to the ground, revealing her rather long tail for all to see. Betty froze.

"Aaargh, no!" she screamed.

Several things then happened all at the same time.

1. Bobby leaped forward to quickly pick the blanket up and cover the unusual protuberance . . .

2. Minnie gave a shriek of surprise and pointed in horror at the large furry tail that had suddenly been revealed . . .

3. And there was a loud clattering and a splash from the direction of Mr. McNumpty's garden.

Chapter 5

Half an hour later, Bobby, Betty and a rather pale Minnie were sitting at the kitchen table in silence and Mrs. Bold was pouring them each some orange juice from a large jug. She had just finished explaining to Minnie the story of who they really were.

She sighed. "So you see, Minnie dear, we Bolds are really hyenas. That's all there is to it. You're such a sweet girl, and have been a very good friend to the twins for a long time, and it felt wrong keeping it a secret from you, so in a way I'm glad you now know."

They all looked at Minnie to see how she might react to the startling news.

After a long, tense pause the color began to return to her cheeks and she broke into a big grin. "Well, goodness me!" she began. "That's the biggest shock ever. I never imagined such a thing! But I guess that does explain why you're always laughing and why you do love wearing hats."

"You're not going to tell, are you?" asked Bobby fearfully. "We might get sent away."

"Please, Minnie," said Betty, holding her hand tightly. "You're my best friend in all the world! Please don't tell anyone, ever!"

"Listen," said Minnie, placing an arm around each of them. "Of course I won't tell! Cross my heart! You two are very special friends.

You always were—and now you are even more special."

The twins and Mrs. Bold all sighed with relief.

"This calls for some cookies!" declared Mrs. Bold, reaching for the cookie tin and placing it on the table. "If only people weren't so peculiar about these things, we honestly wouldn't mind everyone knowing. Maybe one day we will be able to tell the world, but for now we have to keep it under our hats."

"Or in our pants!" quipped Bobby, giving his tail a wiggle.

"I'd love to have a tail," said Minnie. "I honestly would. I'm very envious. They must be such fun."

"Very good for keeping flies away on a hot night," said Betty. "Swoosh your tail around and they're gone."

"I wish I had a secret I could tell you," pondered Minnie. "But I can't think of one. My father was born in Chatham—does that count?"

"Not really, dear," answered Mrs. Bold. "Although I wouldn't tell that to anyone until you know them quite well."

They all sat there chomping happily on their cookies for a moment, until Bobby suddenly dropped his on the plate.

"Goodness!" he cried out. "Mr. McNumpty!"

"What about him?" asked his mother.

"Well, I forgot, what with everything that happened. But he was up his ladder when Betty's tail came out. Supposing he saw everything?"

"Yes, you're right!" said Minnie. "And wasn't there a loud crash? Like he dropped his bucket in surprise?"

"Oh no! Now what shall we do?" wailed Betty.

Mrs. Bold paced up and down for a moment, scratching her head. Eventually she looked at the time on the kitchen clock. "I know," she said. "We'll wait for your father to get home. He won't be long. I expect he'll know what to do about Mr. McNumpty. Minnie dear, you had better run along home soon. Thank you for being such a good friend to the twins. And remember: not a word to anyone."

Like a lot of grown-ups, Mr. Bold was in the habit of bringing his work home with him. This wouldn't be much fun if you were a garbage man or an accountant, but fine if you worked in a chocolate factory or, as was the case with Mr. Bold, you spent your day writing jokes for Christmas crackers. So every day when he got home, it was Mr. Bold's custom to poke his head round the door and tell a joke or two.

Today was no exception.

No sooner had everyone heard his key in the lock and the front door open than his head appeared through the serving hatch to the living room.

Mr. Bold was so happy with his jokes of the day that he always laughed the loudest, even though he had heard them before.

Mrs. Bold waited until Minnie had left and they were all having their tea before she told him about the day's events and the unfortunate appearance of Betty's tail in the garden.

"Minnie is going to keep our secret safe, but we are worried that Mr. McNumpty might have seen the tail and dropped his bucket in surprise. What are we to do?"

"I'll go and talk to him. Man to, er, man," announced Mr. Bold.

"But what if he knows the truth?" asked Betty, feeling a little guilty now that she was the one who had caused all this fuss.

Mr. Bold gave her a gentle pat on the head. "Don't look so worried, sweet pea. Dad to the rescue! If need be, I will have to do that thing that humans do. Lie!" He got up from the dining-room table and rolled up his sleeves.

So Fred Bold marched next door and gave a no-nonsense rap on Mr. McNumpty's door. After a long, meaningful silence the door opened a few inches and the suspicious eye of his neighbor appeared.

"Yes?" he snapped.

"Ah, Mr. McNumpty. Fred from next door. How lovely and clean all your windows are looking! Just checking you are all right . . . my wife tells me there was a bit of a commotion this afternoon."

"Hmph!" came the bad-tempered response.

"We were hoping—I mean, worried—that you'd kicked—I mean dropped the bucket?"

"Still here, aren't I?"

"Good!" said Fred, determined to be jolly friendly whatever response he got from Mr. McNumpty. "Nothing to, er, worry about, then? Just an unfortunate accident?"

"You could say that," hissed Mr. McNumpty. He opened the door wider. "Or maybe I saw something unexpected? Something that made me jump."

"Er . . . I doubt that. Just got a bit giddy up that ladder, didn't you?"

Mr. McNumpty's eyes bulged and he came closer to Fred than was comfortable. "You Bolds had better watch out. Or I might tell . . ."

"Whatever can you mean?" said Fred innocently.

"You know what I mean," came the furious

reply. "Tell TAILS! Yes, TAILS. T-A-I-L-S! You're not right, you lot. Not right at all. I SAW IT!"

"Calm down, old chap," said Fred, holding his hands out as if to protect himself. "Whatever you think you saw, you, er, didn't see at all. That's all there is to it."

"Your daughter has got a tail, and I expect the whole lot of you have. Tails! I knew there was something odd about you Bolds. TAILS!"

"Hush now," said Fred, worried that

Mr. McNumpty's raised voice might be overheard by others in the street. "Of course we don't have tails—I've never heard anything so ridiculous or insulting in my life. What you saw was no such thing."

"It was so!"

"No, no, no, Mr. McNumpty. It was, er, a thing, a furry thing, a toy, yes, that's right. A . . . feather duster!"

"It was a tail that I saw. What are you? Monkeys? Werewolves? I've a good mind to call the ASPCA and have you all taken away."

"Don't do anything silly," said Fred, trying his best to smile endearingly at his angry neighbor, but worrying that his sharp teeth might just add to the man's suspicions. "You're letting your imagination run away with you.

Maybe you have had a bump on the head? Have you got a temperature? Let me feel your forehead . . ." He raised a paw towards Mr. McNumpty, who backed away and almost closed the door completely.

"Get away from me, you beast!"

Fred thought the best thing he could do to calm the situation was say nothing for a moment, so he stood silently and shook his head a little from side to side. "Dear oh dear," he muttered to himself and rolled his eyes. "I admit we are a little . . . unusual," he said reasonably. "But live and let live, eh? And it is nothing like you're saying. My daughter has been very fond of her feather duster since she was a pup—I mean, baby. It's like a comfort blanket to her. Never played with dolls or teddy bears, just that silly feather duster. Now,

let's have no more talk about tails, shall we?"
He gave a gentle laugh.

Mr. McNumpty looked slightly less cross,
as if he was now unsure about what he'd
seen over the fence. "Well, maybe . . ."

"Not maybe, dear chap, definitely," said
Fred conclusively. "I'm terribly sorry if it gave
you a fright and you dropped your bucket."

"But I thought . . ." said Mr. McNumpty,
looking less sure of himself.

"Well, I thought I saw a man in the moon
once, but I didn't at all, did I?" said Fred,
letting out the loud chortle that had been
building up inside him.

"OK," said Mr. McNumpty doubtfully.

"Now. That's that all sorted. Would you like to come in for a cup of tea and some ice cream?" Fred licked his lips encouragingly.

"No, I would not!" said Mr. McNumpty, sounding cross that Fred had managed to talk him out of what he was sure he'd seen. "I keep myself to myself. And be warned, Mr. Bold— I'll be watching you lot. Watching you all very closely indeed. And if I EVER see anything again that makes me think I'm living next door to a bunch of furry critters masquerading as decent law-abiding human beings, I shall blow the whistle on the whole flea-bitten lot of you!"

And with that Mr. McNumpty slammed the door closed.

Chapter 6

Following the fright with Mr. McNumpty, the Bolds were all a little shaken up and they resolved to be more careful. Tails were kept well and truly tucked away, caps and hats were worn at all times to disguise big ears and snouts, and everyone tried not to laugh too loudly in case they annoyed Mr. McNumpty.

Luckily for them, however, Minnie was an understanding, trustworthy friend who kept her word and didn't tell anyone their secret—but they might not be so lucky next time.

You know how it is, though—once a hyena always a hyena. Some things just can't be helped. There was no actual harm in laughing, or indeed scavenging, which comes very naturally to hyenas. But they had to do it on the quiet, that was all, even though it was hard to remember all the time.

Things seemed to be going well until one evening when the Bolds were having their family tea—lamb chops, with chips and some acorns Mrs. Bold had found beneath an oak tree in Bushy Park. Suddenly there was a loud knock at the front door. Betty answered it, and an angry Mr. McNumpty pushed his way past her and into the kitchen.

"You disgust me!" he shouted at Mr. Bold.

"Good evening, Mr. McNumpty," said Mr. Bold politely. "What seems to be the problem?"

"I saw you rubbing your bare bottom on a lilac bush in the garden this morning, that's the problem!" said Mr. McNumpty, getting very red in the face.

Mr. Bold shrugged. "There's no law against that, is there? I was simply marking my territory."

Now I think I'd better explain something here. You've probably heard how dogs mark their territory by weeing over everything. It's a pretty dirty habit, but there are dirtier habits, believe me. Hyenas like to mark their territory too—making their mark

and showing who is boss by wiping their **bottoms** on trees and bushes. It's not very nice, I admit, but there's no harm in it.

Mr. Bold had worked hard at being a human—he wore clothes, cleaned his teeth, used a knife and fork and even read newspapers—but there was one hyena habit he just couldn't give up, no matter how much Mrs. Bold told him not to. He liked rubbing his bottom on plants in the garden to mark his territory. A simple pleasure, but it was going to get him into a lot of **trouble**. But I digress.

"You **filthy** individual!" continued Mr. McNumpty. "And furthermore, your children knocked over my garbage cans."

"No, we didn't!" said the twins in unison.

"No, dear chap," said Mr. Bold. "I'm sorry,

but that was me too. You left a couple of chop bones in there. I could smell them as I passed your cans this morning. Waste not, want not! Delicious!"

Betty looked down at her plate and suddenly lost her appetite.

Mr. McNumpty made a strange growling noise. "Eeeuuurrrgh! You filthy, horrible, revolting lot!" he said. "You live like animals! Why don't you go and live in Kenton Safari Park with all the other beasts? You'd be right at home there!" And with that he left, slamming the door behind him.

The Bolds sat in stunned silence for a moment. Then Mrs. Bold said, "Eat up, children. Anyone for mint sauce?"

"I'm not eating this if it came out of Mr.

McNumpty's garbage," said Betty, wrinkling up her nose.

"All the more for me, then," said her father briskly, taking the plate and scraping the leftovers onto his own. "Back in Africa we wouldn't think twice about it. Everything gets eaten there. Hyenas don't believe in waste!"

"And rubbing your bum on the plants? How could you!" said Betty incredulously.

"Don't say 'bum,' Betty, say 'bottom,'" chipped in Mrs. Bold. Bobby started to laugh.

"How could I? you ask," continued Mr. Bold, chomping on a chop bone. "Very easily, is how. What's wrong with it? We do it all the time back home to leave our calling card. Then when another hyena passes by he knows whose territory it is."

Betty looked as if she might throw up, but Bobby's eyes had definitely lit up at the thought of rubbing his bottom on plants.

"I've done it too," he admitted. "Outside the school gates. I couldn't help myself—it just felt like the right thing to do. No one saw me, though."

"Good boy," said Mr. Bold, now licking the plate with his big hyena tongue. He felt very proud of his son. Rubbing his bottom on plants—Bobby was growing up!

"Thank goodness you weren't spotted, though," said Mrs. Bold, sounding relieved.

Mr. Bold let out an unusually loud laugh. "You see?" he said. "We are hyenas! This is what we do! We laugh, we scavenge—and we rub our bottoms on things!"

"Well, I'm not a scavenger!" said Betty indignantly.

"Yes, you are," corrected her father. "You're a hyena, and don't you forget it."

"Well, dear," said Mrs. Bold, trying to calm things, "I think that's enough for now. We have tried to make our children fit in and act like humans, so please don't confuse matters by telling them it's OK to mark their scent all over the place and rummage through garbage."

Mr. Bold sighed and scratched his head. "You're right, I suppose," he said.

Mrs. Bold leaned over and gave her husband a kiss on his snout. "Are you missing the old country a bit?" she asked quietly.

"Yes, I do miss it and I wish the kids could experience it sometimes. I'm all for them using a knife and fork when we are out to blend in with the humans' funny ways. But we don't need to use them at home, do we? What's the point of cutlery and plates? They should be able to be hyenas sometimes—in the privacy of our own home, surely? I'd like to see them tearing at their meat, scratching themselves and running round the garden with their tails and bottoms out in the fresh air—all the things we did when *we* were growing up!"

The twins looked on, concerned. They had never seen their father so upset and they had never known such a long conversation with no one laughing.

"Are you worried we're forgetting our hyena roots?" asked Bobby.

"Yes, I guess I am," said Mr. Bold. "I'm worried that I am too. Before we know it, you'll be proper human beings who no longer understand animal language and have to rely on supermarkets to feed you."

Now I know you are probably thinking: What is animal language? And what's wrong with getting your food from supermarkets?

And I'm afraid I don't really have the answers for you. I'm not a hyena and neither, presumably, are you.

But the fact is, that as much as Mr. Bold wanted to live as a human, a part of him missed his old life. He would always be a hyena at heart—and he wanted to keep that alive. Deep down, in fact, he wanted to shout about it.

That night, Fred Bold dreamed he was home in Africa, running across the plains, catching antelope for his dinner, wagging his tail wherever he felt like it and laughing long and loud at the top of his hyena voice. He was making such a racket in his sleep that Mrs. Bold was woken up, and she had to jab him several times in the ribs with her paw.

But by the next morning Mr. Bold had formed a plan. He and Mrs. Bold were sitting on deck chairs in the back garden. Bobby, who had been very taken with the idea of marking his scent, was sniffing at a rosebush and trying to resist the temptation to take his trousers down, and Betty and Minnie were flicking through a celebrity magazine, discussing who had the best hairdo.

"I've been thinking," said Mr. Bold to his wife. "I think we need to go back to Africa for a bit. Introduce the kids to their relatives,

let them get back to their hyena roots; have a go at practising their animal language and maybe pick up a few new phrases."

Mrs. Bold laughed. "Darling, I would love to see my family and introduce Betty and Bobby to my parents, but that is the most ridiculous idea I've ever heard! How do you propose we get passports for the children? And what will we do if we can't get back to England? Airport security is very tight these days—supposing they discover our secret and lock us away in a zoo?"

Mr. Bold sighed and shook his head. "Oh dear, I hadn't thought of that," he said. "We can't take that risk."

"No, we certainly can't," agreed Mrs. Bold. "I love our life here in Teddington. I love this house. We love our jobs. And the pups are doing very well at school." (This wasn't strictly true: Bobby had gotten in trouble yet again for laughing all the way through a lesson about the Black Death, but his mother didn't know that.)

"No, I'm sorry, dear," she continued, "but we can't go to Africa, and Africa can't come to us. So we will just have to carry on as we are. It's a good life really."

Minnie, who had been listening to this whole conversation, looked up from her magazine. Something Mrs. Bold said had got her thinking. Animals might be cleverer than human beings, but sometimes human beings can come up with fairly good ideas themselves.

"Er, Mrs. Bold, I think I know a way of bringing Africa to you," she said.

"Do you really, Minnie?" said an astonished Mrs. Bold. "Then let's hear it!"

"It's the school holidays next week, so why don't you go on a trip to Kenton Safari Park? I've seen the posters and their slogan is: *Bringing Africa to you.*"

"That's it! The perfect solution!" said Mr. Bold, jumping out of his deck chair and rolling on the patio, laughing. "And it isn't too far away, either!"

"Well done, Minnie," said Mrs. Bold. "What a clever human being you are!"

All the commotion brought Bobby scampering up the lawn. "What's going on?" he asked.

"We're going on an outing," said Mr. Bold excitedly. "Next week. To the safari park!"

Chapter 7

The following Wednesday the Bolds set off on their expedition to Kenton Safari Park. There would be roller coasters and rides included in the price of the ticket, but the Bolds weren't interested in those. It was the wild animals they wanted to see. For the senior Bolds in particular, this was going to be like a trip home to their motherland.

"We have to stay in the car, dear," Mrs. Bold reminded her husband. "It says so in the brochure. With all the windows wound up. You can't jump out and run rings round the lions like we did in Africa."

"I know, I know," said Mr. Bold a little sadly. "But just the smell of them will be wonderful. There's nothing like the whiff of a lioness, children—pungent and powerful to us hyenas. You'll see."

The twins sat in the back of the car, noses twitching in anticipation, thrilled that they would soon see and smell all the different animals they had only looked at in pictures or on television before. They had never seen their parents in such a tizzy of excitement—and it was catching.

Eventually they arrived at the (to give it its full name) Kenton Wilderness Wildlife Animal Safari Experience.

There was a bit of a line at the main gate, where the park staff sold tickets and explained the rules of the visit.

Stay in your car at all times while in the wilderness area.

Keep all windows and sunroofs firmly shut and don't open them under any circumstances.

Never feed any of the animals.

Never kiss any wild animals.
They don't like it.

(Mrs. Bold said "Pah!" when she heard that one—and Mr. Bold gave her a wink.)

Keep children under control at all times.

If participating in any of our Animal Discovery sessions, do not put hands or fingers in the mouths of animals.

5

> **WASH YOUR HANDS AFTER TOUCHING ALL ANIMALS!**

("And humans, I might add!" whispered Betty.)

> No animals allowed into the park.

(Bobby gave a loud hyena laugh when he heard that!)

Finally they were waved through.

Mrs. Bold squealed with excitement when she looked at the map they had been given. "Oh, goodness me!" she said. "They have every kind of animal here!"

The park was set on hundreds of acres of land where the animals could live and roam very much as they would have done in their natural state. The map showed the road they

100

would drive slowly along and had drawings of each type of animal and where it would be located on the route. There were indeed lots!

Mrs. Bold read the list out, getting louder and more animated as she went: "Lions, tigers, cheetahs, birds of prey, elephants! Monkeys! Parrots! Sea lions! Penguins! Camels and llamas!! Giraffes!! Zebras!! Rhinos!!! Baboons!!! and HYENAS!!!!"

Mr. Bold took out a tissue and offered it to his wife. "You're dribbling, Amelia," he said.

"Oh!" she replied, and wiped the drool from her chin.

"I want to see the lions first!" said Bobby, who had been very patient during the journey. Now they were finally in the park, he couldn't hold it in any longer.

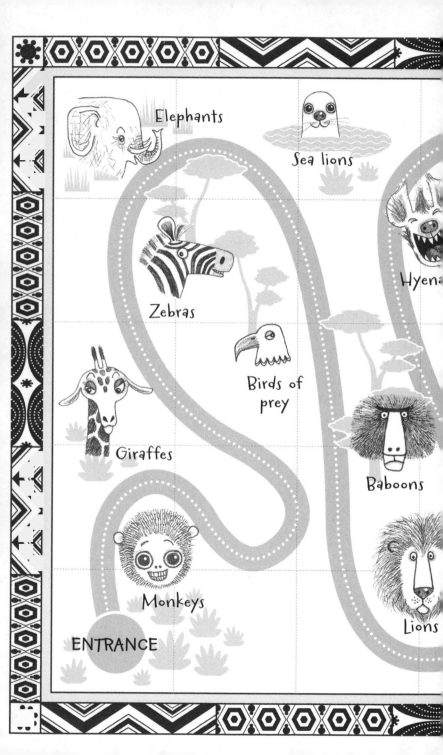

"Rhinos! Rhinos!" shouted Betty.

"Calm yourselves, children," said Mrs. Bold. "We have to drive slowly along this road and we will see all the animals as we go. It's not a zoo where we can go and look at them in cages." She glanced back down at the map. "According to this, we will see the monkeys first."

"Right. If we're all ready?" said Mr. Bold, driving towards the final set of gates into the wilderness area. "We just have time for a quick joke."

How do monkeys get down the stairs?

They slide down the banana-ster!

The children laughed, and Mrs. Bold gave Mr. Bold a playful slap on his arm.

And then they drove through the gates and past a big red sign warning them that monkeys could damage their car and the safari park would take no responsibility.

At first nothing much happened. The monkeys were nowhere to be seen.

"Is that one up that tree there?" asked Mrs. Bold.

"Maybe," said Mr. Bold doubtfully. Then he cocked his ear and said, "Ssssh! Can you hear that?" To begin with, it was just a high-pitched sound, a bit like a seagull. But then it got louder and louder—a chattering, clattering, happy sound that seemed to echo all around them.

Mrs. Bold turned round to Bobby and Betty. Her face was filled with happiness. "That sound, children? It's the monkeys—they are greeting us!"

A loud thud made her jump back round.

"There's one on the roof!" laughed Mr. Bold. The noise got even louder and there were more thuds. Then a monkey—a flash of brown fur and teeth—landed on the bonnet of their car. Then another, and another. Their smiling monkey faces peered through the windows and the monkeys on the roof appeared upside down at the passenger windows. They all shrieked their welcome over and over again.

"Thank you, monkeys!" said Mrs. Bold, dabbing her eyes with a hankie. Then both she and Mr. Bold began to make noises of their own that weren't any words Bobby or Betty

had ever heard before. They both cackled and whooped in reply to the monkeys, who made similar noises back to them. More and more monkeys came and jumped on the car, some of them pressing their monkey mouths to the windows and blowing noisy raspberries at the Bolds.

"Bless them, the darlings!" said Mrs. Bold, talking in English again. "They know we are animals and they are saying hello."

Suddenly a big, black-and-white striped Land Rover full of safari park rangers pulled alongside the Bolds' car and sounded a loud siren a bit like a ship's foghorn. The monkeys all scampered away and climbed back up into the trees.

"Move along, please!" the rangers told Mr. Bold through a loudspeaker. "The monkeys

108

are a little over-friendly today, nothing
to be alarmed about."

"Oh, we're not alarmed!" replied Mr. Bold.
"We were rather enjoying all the attention."

"Wowsers," said Betty. "That was amazeballs."

"Which animals are next?" asked Bobby.

"Giraffes and zebras," said Mr. Bold, without
even glancing at the map. "I can smell them,
can't you?"

The twins sniffed the air. They had no idea what giraffes or zebras smelled like, but they inhaled some horsey, straw-like scents that were entirely new to them.

"I can smell something interesting!" said Bobby.

"OMG," agreed Betty. "Delish!"

Several giraffes were loitering a few yards from the road, chewing some leaves from the top of a tree. They swung their heads to stare as the Bolds' car approached, but they didn't move.

"Hello, giraffes!" said Mrs. Bold. "Come and say hello, why don't you?" The giraffes stopped chewing and looked decidedly outraged at Mrs. Bold's suggestion.

110

A herd of zebras was next. They all raised their heads from where they were grazing, took one look at the Bolds' vehicle, seemed to look at each other in amazement for a moment, and then galloped away quickly in the opposite direction, a cloud of dust at their hooves.

"Why, it's as if they want to get away from us!" said Bobby.

"Yes, what's their problem?" asked Betty.

"Well, dears," said Mrs. Bold, glancing back to make sure the park rangers weren't watching all the different reactions this particular carload of visitors was getting from the park inhabitants, "hyenas and zebras never were the best of friends in Africa."

"Personality clash?" asked Betty.

"Like Mr. McNumpty?" asked Bobby.

"Something like that," said Mrs. Bold.

"Well, what?" persisted Bobby. "We're only looking at them, like everyone else."

Mr. Bold sighed. "It's just that where we came from, well, there weren't any shops, you see. So we hyenas would get a bit peckish. And . . ."

"And what?" demanded Betty.

"Well, how can I put this?" he stuttered.

"Hyenas find zebras quite tasty," said Mrs. Bold in a sudden rush.

"Yuck!" said Betty.

"Well, they needn't worry about us," laughed Bobby. "We're going to the Wilderness Café for our lunch today."

"Quite," said Mrs. Bold. "Now, what's next?" She consulted the map. "Ah, elephants." She sounded relieved. There wouldn't be too much reaction from the elephants. These huge, graceful creatures were not bothered by anything or anyone much, on the plains of the Serengeti. (Apart from evil poachers, of course.)

A large family of elephants glided past the car, their big, knowing eyes looking a little surprised as they spotted the Bolds—but there was no other reaction. The Bolds all agreed they were magnificent, majestic animals.

"My favorite so far," declared Bobby.

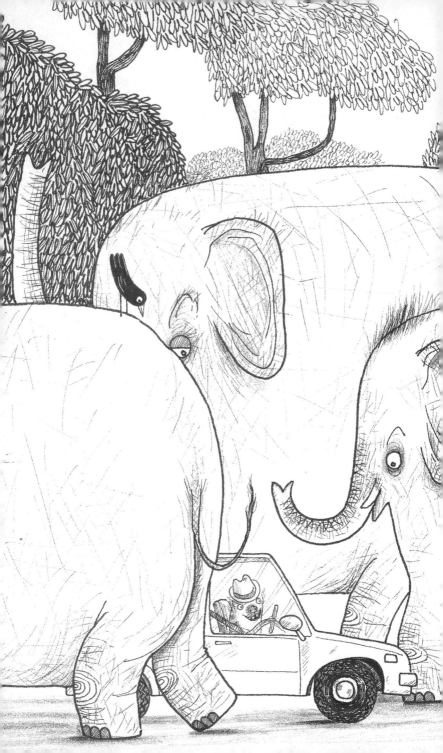

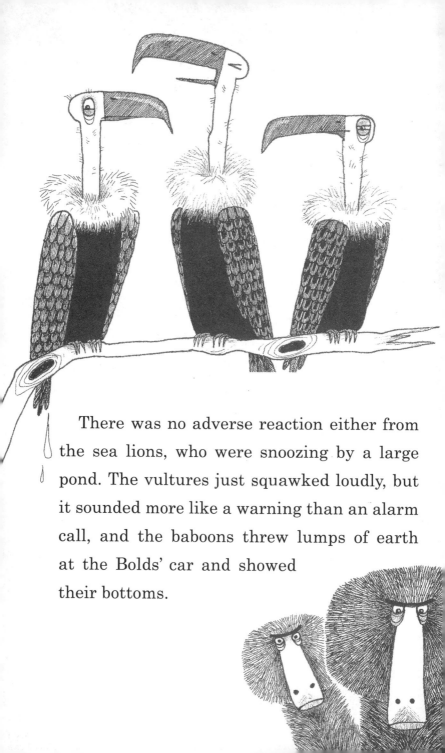

There was no adverse reaction either from the sea lions, who were snoozing by a large pond. The vultures just squawked loudly, but it sounded more like a warning than an alarm call, and the baboons threw lumps of earth at the Bolds' car and showed their bottoms.

"Gross!" said Betty.

But then they got to the wild cats.

"Lions next," said Mrs. Bold, glancing nervously at her husband. "Do you think we should turn back?"

"Why, Mum?" asked Bobby innocently. "I want to see the lions, the kings of the jungle!"

"Lions and hyenas don't get on, dear," said Mrs. Bold. "In fact, we're archenemies. Are your windows firmly shut?"

"Oh," replied Bobby excitedly. "Is there going to be a rumble in the jungle?"

"With any luck they'll be asleep," Mr. Bold reassured him.

"We're not in Africa now, are we?" said Betty reasonably.

"You can take the lion out of the wild, but you can't take the wild out of the lion," said Mr. Bold sagely.

A pride of about ten lions of all shapes and sizes was lying on the grass, dozing in the summer sunshine. At least, they were until they got wind of the Bolds' car. One by one they stood up, staring intently at the blue Honda. Betty gave a **nervous** giggle as two lionesses crouched down low and began to creep towards the car.

"Do you think we should speed up a bit, Dad?" asked Bobby. By now a huge male lion was joining in, baring his teeth as he crept along. Mr. Bold accelerated, but already the three lions were in full pursuit, **hissing** and **spitting** at the Bolds with hatred in their eyes, the muscles in their backs rippling as they gathered pace towards their prey.

"Quick!" said Bobby, "They're nearly upon us!"

"Uh-oh," said Mr. Bold. "There's only one thing to do in a situation like this. Ready, Amelia?"

"Ready," said Mrs. Bold through gritted teeth.

Mr. Bold slammed on the brakes, and both he and Mrs. Bold opened their windows. Just as the nearest lioness was about to pounce on the car, the senior Bolds began a loud cackling and screaming—a cross between a laugh and a yell. The lions all stopped in their tracks, hesitated, hissed violently and then turned and fled.

Mr. and Mrs. Bold stopped their noises and wound up the windows.

"Shall we proceed, dear?" said Mrs. Bold with a prim smile, and Mr. Bold carried on with his driving.

"Yes," he said. "Let's."

The twins looked at each other in astonishment.

"What was THAT all about?" asked Betty.

"Oh, the noise we made?" said Mrs. Bold. "Just an old trick from the mother country."

"Sounded wicked!" said Bobby, immediately trying to make a similar cacophony but sounding more like an angry parrot.

"That's enough, Bobby. You haven't quite got the hang of it. I'll teach you how to do it properly when we are somewhere far away from anyone who might hear," said his father. "It is the hyena war cry—only to be used in situations of extreme danger or combat. Usually does the trick! Now then, what's next?"

"Oooh, Fred!" exclaimed Amelia after consulting the map. "The hyenas are next. The moment we have all been waiting for!"

Chapter

It comes as no surprise to me that animals can talk. I'd be more surprised if they couldn't. I have always talked to my pets and felt sure that they understood me. And I don't just mean "Good boy" and "Bad boy." The other day I had a very interesting conversation with my dog Albert about classical music. My favorite composer is Mozart. He said Bach.

All living things communicate. Even members of the royal family know this—apparently they chat to their plants. Mainly rhubarb.

When humans talk to animals it is one thing, but when animals talk to each other it is very hard to keep up—it's like listening to a foreign language. Which, of course, it is. Dogs bark to each other over the garden fence—"Woof, woof, woof!"—but we can only guess what they are on about. Goldfish open and close their mouths, but we can't hear a word. Only other goldfish understand.

As the Bolds entered the hyena enclosure at Kenton Safari Park, the conversation between Mr. and Mrs. Bold and the "resident" hyenas was really quite advanced, as far as animal conversation goes.

The safari hyenas didn't speak English, although they understood it, so I think it will be easiest if I just translate it all for you—otherwise it will just be a lot of "grrrumps" and "shhrrrieekkks!" which wouldn't be much fun for you to read, nor would it make any sense whatsoever.

Bobby and Betty—although they hadn't been taught much hyena language—instinctively understood the general gist of everything that was said because they actually *were* hyenas. But I know and can translate for you because I'm very clever, and that's all I can say on the matter. Now, let's get on with the story.

Ah, but before we do, I need to explain a couple of things. There was a clan of six hyenas living at Kenton Safari Park: a couple named Boo and Ena, their three young pups born that spring, and a gnarled, elderly male named Tony.

They had a nice life, with plenty of fresh meat thrown to them by the keepers, a warm burrow to sleep in at night, and plenty of space to run

around in. They didn't even mind the endless stream of cars driving past or the people inside leering at them. Boo and Ena would sometimes put on a bit of a show, running around chasing their tails or doing loud hyena laughs, which seemed to amuse the human visitors. They were protective of their three pups when they were first born, but proudly showed them off now they were a bit older.

However, Tony—the older male—was feeling his age. He had a touch of arthritis and mostly lay about in the shade dozing, although he managed to get to his feet when it was feeding time.

All of the hyenas knew their keeper well, and the evening before the Bold family visit, feeding time had taken place, as usual, at six o'clock. The hyenas were always ready for their food and would pace up and down the fence of their enclosure waiting for the truck to arrive. The keeper would then throw tasty chunks of meat through a specially designed hatch. Yesterday, though, there had been someone else with her: the vet. As the hyenas tucked into their dinner they could see the vet watching them and taking notes. This in itself was not that unusual: since the pups had been born the vet often came to take a look and check that they were healthy and happy.

But this time the vet was clearly interested in Tony, and he was writing things down on a clipboard.

"What's with the vet?" Boo asked Ena.

"Who knows?" replied Ena. "Seems to be watching Tony very closely. Have you noticed, Tony?"

Tony couldn't see or hear particularly well at his age—but he knew when he was being watched. "Nosy parkers," he muttered with his mouth full. "Making a note of my middle-age spread, I shouldn't wonder. How rude of them!" Tony had been at the safari park for many years, and used to be the leader of the hyenas. But nowadays he enjoyed his quiet life. He finished his dinner and dozed off to sleep.

Boo and Ena were licking the pups' faces clean when they heard the vet say to the keeper, "It's very sad, but I think it's time we put the old hyena to sleep. He's a tired, grey-haired old fella, and that arthritis is clearly paining him and causing him a lot of trouble. Very soon the other hyenas will turn on him and kill him. It happens in the wild, and I don't want it happening here. I think we should put him out of his misery."

131

"OK," said the keeper. "It's for the best. We've got a lot of tourists coming this week, so let's do it . . . next Wednesday, after the park has closed for the day?"

"Right-o," agreed the vet, making a note of the date on his clipboard. "Sad, isn't it?"

"He's had a good run," said the keeper. "Been here longer than me. But he won't feel a thing, will he?"

"No, not at all. See you next week."

Boo and Ena stopped what they were doing, horrified.

"No!" said Ena. "Not Tony—they can't!"

"There's nothing wrong with him—he's just old! He grumbles a bit about his arthritis, but he's definitely not in constant pain and there's no way we'd ever attack and kill him. How could they say such a thing?" said Boo. They looked over to where Tony was sleeping, happily oblivious.

"We must try and stop them," Ena said. "But how?"

"There's nothing we can do, I'm afraid," said Boo. "Once their minds are made up, that's it. Poor Tony."

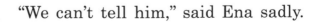 "We can't tell him," said Ena sadly.

"We must let him live out his last few days happy and content."

And they both resolved to be especially nice to Tony, giving him the finest bits of meat to eat and letting him sleep in the most comfortable spot in the burrow.

He only had another seven days!

Chapter 9

The chatter in the Bolds' car was at **fever pitch** as they entered the hyena enclosure in the park.

"My tail is wagging inside my trousers like no one's business," said Mr. Bold. "I just can't believe we are going to see some of our brothers and sisters at long last."

"Can we get out the car and play with them?" asked Bobby.

"Unfortunately not, dear," said his mother.

"The rules are very strict about that. But isn't it exciting?"

"I've never even seen another hyena," said Betty. "Apart from us. What shall I say to them?"

"We will use animal language," said Mr. Bold firmly.

"I expect it will come naturally to you," added Mrs. Bold. "Once you hear it."

Did you hear about the hyena who drank a pint of gravy?

He made a laughing stock of himself!

"Look!" shouted Bobby. "There they are!"

The hyenas were about fifty yards ahead, not far from the road. Tony was lying on his back and the pups were climbing all over him, nuzzling his whiskered face and tumbling onto the grass before jumping back onto his stomach. Tony was smiling at them indulgently, occasionally giving each pup an affectionate lick, while Boo and Ena sat side by side a few yards away, looking on proudly but checking that the pups' game didn't get too boisterous for Tony.

"They've got babies!" said Betty. "Three of them! That's just so cute."

137

Unable to contain their excitement any longer, Fred and Amelia began shouting their greetings. "Hello! Over here! In the Honda!" and, "Don't give the game away, but we are hyenas too!"

Boo turned to the Bolds' car, looking confused. Had he really heard hyena voices? Then he saw them.

"Don't look now, Ena, but there's a car full of hyenas dressed as people," he said.

"You're having a giraffe," said Ena, peering towards the Honda. "Good heavens," she stammered. "I do believe you're right . . ." They both blinked their eyes in astonishment.

"Yoo hoo!" shouted Fred. "We are so pleased to see you. Are you OK?"

Ena and Boo shouted to Tony to stay with the pups and then they ran closer to the Bolds for a better look.

"What on earth . . . ?" said Boo. "Yes, you really are hyenas!"

"I've never seen such a thing!" said Ena. "Who are you? Where are you from? How come . . . ?"

"It's a long story, friends," said Fred, quickly introducing himself, Amelia, and the children. "But we came here from Africa a few years back. Found some passports . . . Now we live in disguise. We've even got jobs and—"

"I've got an overwhelming urge to get out of the car and sniff some hyena bottoms," interrupted Bobby.

"You'd be very welcome to," said Boo. "We do it all the time. But I don't think the keepers would like it."

"No, Bobby," said Mrs. Bold. "We must stay in the car."

"This is my Boo, and I'm Ena," said Ena.

"Hi, Ena," said Fred. "Hyena! That's funny!"

"Oh yes," agreed Ena. "Never fails!" And everyone had a jolly good, loud laugh.

Everyone—both clans—had so much to talk about, all of them amazed to meet some other hyenas. After a while, Ena called the pups over to meet their new friends, and Tony also ambled over, scratching his head at the sight of the Bolds.

"Living in a house? Sounds very nice," he said. "It gets a bit cold here in the safari park in winter time. In fact, I think I've got a touch of arthritis in my back legs."

"Still, we mustn't grumble," said Boo. "We're looked after very well here. Nice food delivered to us already cut up at six o'clock on the dot every day."

"If you'll excuse me," said Tony, "I've got a call of nature to make." He wandered off into the long grass to attend to it.

"What a sweet, adorable chap," said Mrs. Bold.

"He's like the granddad we never had," said Bobby as he watched Tony limp off.

"It's all so sad though," said Ena, her voice quivering with emotion. "His days are numbered."

"Why is that?" asked Mr. Bold.

Ena couldn't bring herself to tell the story, so Boo took over.

"The vet says Tony is too old. Thinks his arthritis is too painful. But the worst thing is, they think that because he's weak Ena and I will attack him. But we'd never do that. He's practically family, and our pups adore him. But . . ." He drew his claw across his throat. "Next Wednesday."

"No!" said Betty, horrified. "They're going to kill him?"

"Well, yes, put him to sleep. We heard them talking about it yesterday."

"Tony doesn't know he's a condemned hyena," said Ena. "We thought it best not to tell him. It's too awful—he's such a lovely, kind old dear."

"And they are putting him down just because he's a bit past it?" asked Mr. Bold. "That's terrible."

"Can't we take him home to live with us?" asked Betty.

"How can we, dear?" said Mr. Bold. "This is a safari park—not a rescue center for homeless animals."

Just then the keepers' Land Rover drew alongside the Bolds' Honda. For the park hyenas to spend so long next to one car was a cause for concern, and they told the Bolds to move along and make sure their windows were up.

Mr. Bold rubbed his chin for a moment. "We have to go," he called as he began to edge the car away. "But listen. Maybe, just maybe, I can think of a way to help poor Tony and save him from the fate that awaits him next Wednesday."

Boo and Ena yelped with relief.

"I can't promise, but let me think of something. I will come back and tell you what the plan is when I've had time to work something out!"

Everyone howled their hyena good-byes and the Bolds drove on.

Chapter
10

The effect of meeting some other hyenas and, more particularly, the fact that Tony—the older hyena—was going to be put to sleep, had made the Bolds very thoughtful by the time they got home that day.

"I thought it would be fun," said Mr. Bold, "but now I'm not so sure." It was certainly no laughing matter.

"Wonderful as it was to meet some animals the same as us, I don't feel particularly happy now," said Mrs. Bold.

"Human beings are horrible!" cried Betty. "How can they do such a terrible thing to Tony?"

"I don't want to live like a human being if that's what they are like," said Bobby crossly. "I'd rather go back to the wild."

But luckily a clever hyena plan had been whirring around in Mr. Bold's brain on the drive back and he had perhaps, perhaps, thought of a way to save Tony and cheer everyone up in the process.

"How would you feel," he asked, "if Tony came to live with us?"

"Oh, yes!" said the twins. "Yes please!"

"But what do you mean, dear?" asked Amelia. "How could he?"

148

"Well, it isn't going to be easy. But I think there is a way we could rescue him. Now. Have we still got the map of the safari park?"

Mrs. Bold took it out of her handbag and passed it to him.

Mr. Bold spread it out on the table and studied it carefully. "Hmmm. I see," he said. "We only have a week, so we'd better act fast. And we're going to need the help of Minnie. Betty, give her a call and see if she can come over tomorrow morning. This evening we will clean out the spare bedroom, which is full of junk, old sticks, and half-chewed bones. The next few days are going to be very busy indeed. Just as well it's the school holidays. And we're going to be working in the dead of night, so I'm afraid no one is going to be getting much sleep."

Fred took the next few days off work to carry out his plan. First he drove back to the safari park in the morning and told Ena and Boo the details—and they were so *excited* they jumped somersaults.

"It's quite *brilliant!*" they laughed and chortled.

"But you need to talk to Tony," said Fred. "If he isn't happy about coming to live with us Bolds, then we can't really do it."

"But the alternative is too awful," said Ena.

"And he can come and see you whenever he feels like it," added Fred.

"Right," said Boo. "I like that idea. Because we are going to miss him here."

So what exactly was Mr. Bold's plan? I hear you asking. Well, it involved digging. LOTS of digging. At night. The Bolds were going to dig a tunnel from outside the safari park. Mr. Bold had chosen an area by the perimeter that was sheltered by some trees and scrubby bushes so no one would notice. Meanwhile Ena and Boo would dig from inside their burrow, unseen by the keepers. All being well, the two tunnels would meet halfway, Tony could escape, and then the tunnels could be filled in. By the time the safari park keepers arrived for work next Wednesday, the tunnel would be gone and Tony would be warm and cozy in the Bolds' spare room!

"But then what?" asked Amelia. "Once they discover Tony has gone missing there will be terrible trouble: headline news, HYENA ON THE LOOSE! There will be house-to-house searches and everything! We could all be in danger!"

Fred had thought of this too, and that's where Minnie came in. Her father, you might remember, was a butcher on Teddington High Street. So Minnie's task was to get some big bones from the fridge storeroom at the back of the shop that could then be strewn around the hyenas' enclosure. Then the keepers, discovering Tony was missing, would put two and two together and make five, and assume that Tony had been eaten by the other hyenas, just as they'd predicted. It might seem a little grisly to you as a human being, but not as grisly as what the vet (a human) was planning to do to poor Tony (a hyena).

The whole, unsavory business would be hushed up, and no unnecessary publicity would result. A spot of cannibalism among wild animals isn't unheard of, and they would quite reasonably think nature had simply taken its course.

That was the plan, anyway. But could it really work? Fred didn't know, but it was the best plan he had. In fact, it was the only plan he had.

The digging began that very night. Long after most people had gone to bed, all four Bolds crept out of the house and got in the car.

Now for you and me, being up all night would feel very odd indeed, but in actual fact hyenas are nocturnal. Like owls and bats, they like to sleep during the day and go out and about under cover of darkness. This was another habit the Bolds had had to break when they arrived in Teddington, in order not to draw too much attention to themselves as they pretended to be humans. But they now slipped easily back into being awake at night as their journey to the safari park started. And so too did Betty and Bobby.

At the sound of the car engine starting, a light went on upstairs in Mr. McNumpty's house and his big, cross face appeared at the window, peering out at them and scowling. For some reason he was a touch nocturnal himself.

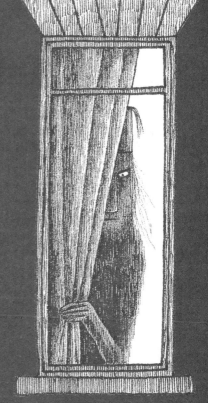

"Poo," said Mr. Bold. "We've been spotted. Never mind. No law against going out after dark."

The Bolds drove to Kenton and parked by the high wall at the back of the safari park. Checking no one was about, they scuttled to the chosen spot, hidden behind a thick covering of ferns and brambles.

"What now?" asked an excited Bobby.

"Listen, everyone," said Mr. Bold, as he consulted the safari park map. "This is where the hard work begins. The hyena burrow is exactly sixty yards in that direction." He signalled to the other side of the wall. "And we've got to dig down and then across. Boo and Ena will do the same from their side—they tell me they are very good at digging, so they can do as much as we do every night. Tonight is Thursday. We have to get five yards along every night, and so do they—though they can do some digging in the daytime too, if they're careful not to be seen. By my calculations we should meet in the middle sometime on Tuesday night at the latest. Then we can get Tony out."

"We hyenas are very good at digging," added Mrs. Bold reassuringly. "And there are four of us, so we can take it in shifts."

"Does this mean I've got to get dirty?" asked Betty, wrinkling up her nose.

"Yes, sweetness," said Mr. Bold, rolling up his sleeves. "Covered in muck and dirt from head to paw."

"Digging is second nature to us. You'll love it once you get going," Mrs. Bold reassured her daughter.

"Gross!" said Betty.

"Let's do this thing!" said Bobby, chuckling.

Mr. Bold spent a minute choosing the right spot to start the tunnel, and then got down on all fours. With his front paws he began to scratch at the ground, moving leaves and twigs to one side. Then, pressing harder, he started to dig. The top soil was dry and powdery, but once he got into his rhythm it became dark and damp and big clods of earth were loosened and removed. Then he started in earnest, head to the ground, his front legs digging faster and faster until they became a blur, and out behind him, from between his hind legs came a spray of earth and sand, like a garden hose at full blast. And slowly, as the hole he created got bigger, his head and shoulders disappeared from view.

After ten minutes he stopped for a break, reversing back out. His snout was covered in earth and he was panting for breath, his big pink tongue lolling out the side of his mouth. He'd never looked less like a human and more like a hyena—Mrs. Bold thought him very attractive.

"Here, dear," she said coquettishly, pouring a bottle of water into a bowl and placing it on the ground. "Have a drink. In the old-fashioned

way, for once." Mr. Bold got down and lapped at the water like a thirsty dog (or hyena).

"Wow, Dad!" said Betty. "You look wild!"

"That felt good!" panted Mr. Bold. "Who wants a go?"

"Me please!" said Bobby. His paws had been twitching to have a good dig the moment he saw his father start.

"Off you go, then," said Mrs. Bold. "Hop in."

Bobby gave a yelp of excitement and leaped into the hole. It was as exhilarating as riding a bike for the first time, and he took to it like a duck to water.

A few hours later, all four Bolds were covered in mud—filthy, tired, but gloriously happy.

Even Betty had loved her first digging experience—giving way to her hyena instincts for once had been deeply satisfying.

"Who knew?" she said, admiring the black earth beneath her fingernails. "It's more fun than anything else, ever!"

"I want to be a professional digger when I grow up," announced Bobby.

They had dug the first five yards of the tunnel, and as the dawn was beginning to break, Mr. Bold said it was time to go home.

"We've made a good start," he told his family. "And we'll be back to dig some more tomorrow."

"Bath and breakfast!" said Mrs. Bold.

"That reminds me . . ."

Chapter 11

For us humans, it is difficult to understand how wonderful the feral activity of getting down and dirty was for the Bolds. Although they were on a mission to save poor Tony, the nightly visit to the tunnel and the frantic digging and getting covered in muck and filth was, to them, a form of liberation: like a caged bird suddenly being allowed to fly free in the endless sky.

The Bolds were happier than they could have ever imagined—the only sad part was washing off all the mud when they got home each morning. Bobby and Betty had to be reminded to walk primly on their hind legs again, and Mr. Bold had to stop himself from rubbing his rump on the garden gate.

The only worry was the troublesome Mr. McNumpty, who not only seemed to observe them leaving the house late each night, but also saw them returning, caked in dry mud. But Mr. Bold knew there was nothing they could do about their nosy neighbor. What they did was their own business, and Mr. McNumpty could be as curious as he wanted—he would never know what they had been up to.

The tunnel, meanwhile, was progressing according to Fred's plan. It was, roughly speaking, a round tube, about a yard and a half in diameter. Some tree roots dangled down in places, water trickled in and formed puddles, moles peeked in though the walls occasionally, wondering what was going on, but it seemed sturdy enough. After all, it only had to last a couple more days, and then Tony could

be transported out of the safari park to the safety of Fairfield Road.

On Monday afternoon Mr. Bold visited the safari park again, and Boo and Ena (whom he had to wake up by beeping his horn, because they were so tired from their nightly exertions) said things were going excellently from their end too. If everything went according to plan the two tunnels should join up on Tuesday night.

Tony came up to speak to Fred too.

"Thank you," he said, his eyes watery with emotion. "From the bottom of my heart. I promise I will be no trouble to you and your family. What you're doing for me is so kind . . . I can't think how I can ever repay you. But . . . you don't think anything could go wrong, do you?" He looked worried.

Fred shook his head reassuringly. "Don't you worry about a thing, Tony. It's all under control and we're looking forward to having you. You will have a lovely life with us. We've got the spare room all ready for you—a nice comfy bed, litter tray, dog biscuits—you'll be very happy, I promise!"

It was Tuesday afternoon, and not long before the night of the final dig, when the two tunnels should meet and Tony could make his escape. By now Mr. McNumpty was convinced there was something very *sinister* going on with his next-door neighbors. What possible explanation could there be for such strange nocturnal activities? Grave robbers? he wondered darkly. He even went to the local cemetery to see if there was any evidence, but there was no sign of anything much. Mr. Bold was right, though—there was no law against going out at night, and there wasn't anything Mr. McNumpty could do about it.

That afternoon Minnie came over dragging a large black garbage bag.

"I got as many big bones as I could," she said, a little breathlessly. "From the back room at my dad's shop, where they cut all the meat up."

Mr. Bold peered inside and licked his lips. There were big, juicy bones and ribs, perfect for fooling the safari park keepers.

"Well done, Minnie," he said, restraining himself from having a quick nibble. "They'll think this is all that's left of poor Tony." He placed the garbage bag carefully by the front door. "I think this calls for a few butcher jokes . . . Listen up, everyone." He cleared his throat and waited until everyone was listening eagerly.

What happened when the butcher backed into the bacon slicer?

He got a little behind with his work!

Everyone laughed heartily and asked for another joke.

"Er, let me see," said Mr. Bold. "Ah, yes!"

Two butchers in a kayak were a bit chilly, so they lit a fire and the kayak sank.

Which just goes to show, doesn't it? You can't have your kayak and heat it too!

Before the Bolds left for the final dig that night, Fred gathered them all around the kitchen table and checked the time.

What does a clock do when it's hungry?

Goes back four seconds!

Betty and Bobby giggled. "No, seriously," their father continued. "We're nearly home and dry, folks. All being well, in a few hours' time our work will be done and we will be welcoming a new member to our family."

"Hurrah!" said Bobby.

"Yes, indeed," said Mr. Bold. "But I just want to run through a few things. Firstly, poor Tony is a hyena like us, but he hasn't yet learned to disguise this fact. We need to be careful—we are being watched, and I think you know to whom I am referring?"

"Nosy McNumpty!" said Betty without hesitation.

"Yes!" said Mr. Bold. His eyes began to twinkle, which usually meant he was about to tell another joke.

What do you call a man whose neighbor takes his tools?

A saw loser!

"Oh really, Fred," said Mrs. Bold, smiling. "This is no joking matter!"

"Sorry, couldn't resist!" said Mr. Bold. "Seriously, though, we shall have to keep our curtains drawn, and Tony mustn't go for a run about in the garden unless we are sure the coast is clear. Understood?"

"Yes, sir!" said the twins.

"Mr. McNumpty knows we are up to something, so we have to be extra-careful."

"And it's going to take poor Tony a while to adjust," added Mrs. Bold. "He is old and probably wise, but he has never lived in a house before. We must be patient and understanding with him. He'll need, er, toilet training, among other things."

Mr. Bold nodded in agreement, then said:

Why did the toilet paper roll down the hill?

To get to the bottom!

"Ha ha!" said Bobby.

"Want another one?" asked his father.

"Oh, go on then," said Mrs. Bold. "But quickly, then we really must be off."

"Here goes!" said Fred.

Some thieves broke into a police station and stole the toilet.

The police are investigating, but for now they've got nothing to go on.

Boom boom!

A short while later, carrying the garbage bag full of bones and the flashlight, they set off, Mr. McNumpty glowering at them from his bedroom window.

There was a thunderstorm going on that night, so the work was even muddier than usual. It was particularly tough going, and all the Bolds were exhausted. After two hours of digging, taking turns every ten minutes, all four Bolds were down in the tunnel together, streaked with glistening mud and sweat, their clothes soaked and clinging to them.

Then they heard a noise.

"Hush!" said Mr. Bold suddenly. "What's that?" He shone the flashlight around the walls of the tunnel, and then they heard it again, a faint scratching noise coming from right ahead of them.

"This is it! We're nearly through!" he whispered. "Look!"

The wall of earth crumbled slightly before their eyes and the scratching sounded louder.

"Boo? Ena?" Mr. Bold called. "It's Fred!"

The scratching stopped and a faint "Hello!" could be heard.

"Stand back!" said Mr. Bold and he began scraping frantically at the earth for a few minutes—until suddenly a hole appeared and a big brown eye looked through at them.

"Who's there?" asked Mr. Bold.

"Boo!"

"Boo who?"

"Boo!"

Mr. Bold couldn't help himself. "Boo hoo! Don't cry, I didn't mean to scare you," he joked.

Bobby snorted with laughter.

"It's Boo, silly!" said Betty.

"Yes, of course it is! Who did you think it was? The Prime Minister?" panted Boo.

"We've done it!" cried Bobby.

Mrs. Bold was almost in tears with

excitement. Within moments the hole was big enough for Boo, Ena, and then (with a few moans and groans) poor Tony to climb through, and although it was a tight squeeze they all slipped about hugging each other and congratulating themselves.

In the confusion there was even a bit of bottom-sniffing going on, but all of the hyenas were so euphoric, who could blame them?

"There is no time to lose," said Mr. Bold, once the greetings were over. "Tony had better say his good-byes and then we'll get him into the car and away to Fairfield Road."

The Bolds all stood respectfully while Boo and Ena walked over to Tony.

"We will miss you more than you will ever know," said Ena, tenderly licking his face.

"Me too," said Tony, holding back his tears. "Tell the pups I love them, and will be along to see them soon."

Boo was next. He nuzzled him in a manly way. "Good-bye, old fella," he said. "We'll be seeing you."

"We'll look after him, don't you worry!" Mrs. Bold said.

Mr. Bold passed Boo the garbage bag full of bones. "Chew on these a bit," he instructed. "Then scatter them around the enclosure. With any luck the keepers will think you've eaten poor Tony."

"Never mind about our reputation!" sniffed Ena, although her mouth was watering at the thought of all those tasty bones to gnaw on.

"It was the best idea I could come up with!" said Mr. Bold. "Now, quickly, Tony, come with us! Remember, you two—block up the tunnel at your end as soon as you get back." His plan was to guide Tony along the tunnel to the entrance, then bundle him into an old sack and into the car—in case anyone was passing and thought a hyena walking along the sidewalk was suspicious.

Tony turned to take a last look at Boo and

Ena, but just at that moment the flashlight flickered and then died, plunging everyone into darkness.

"Oh no!" groaned Betty. "Now we can barely see a thing."

"Don't panic," said Mr. Bold. "There's only one direction we can go in—we can hardly get lost! Come on, everyone."

The Bolds and Tony went in one direction, while Boo and Ena returned to the hyena enclosure in the opposite direction, with the garbage bag full of bones.

But just as the Bolds and Tony neared the end there was a sinister rumbling noise from above them, and clods of damp earth began falling on everyone's heads.

"Who's throwing things?" asked Mrs. Bold. "This is no time for games."

"Oh no, it's not that," said Mr. Bold breathlessly. "It's the tunnel—I think it's collapsing! The rain has soaked the earth and made it much heavier. We must be quick!"

At that moment a huge lump the size of a football fell from the ceiling and landed on poor Tony's shoulder.

"Ouch!" groaned Tony and he began to pant. The cascade of mud, earth, and dirty brown water continued to plop all around him.

"I can reach the ceiling if I stand on tiptoe," said Betty to her father. "Bobby, you do the same. We can hold the ceiling up while you get Tony out. Be quick, though!"

Bobby reached up and it was true—with their paws spread out they could both hold up a small part of the slimy, wet roof of the tunnel.

"I can feel it moving and cracking," gasped Bobby. "Hurry!"

Hyenas can see more in the dark than humans, but muddy water was now stinging everyone's eyes and the trickle through the twins' paws was fast becoming a torrent.

"I'm frightened," whimpered Tony, who hadn't left the safety of the hyena enclosure for many years and was now wishing he was back there.

"We'll help you, Tony," said Mrs. Bold. "Fred, you pull him from the front and I'll push from the back."

"Please hurry!" said Bobby.

"Dudes, this tunnel is nearly busted," said Betty, her voice weak with the strain of holding up the heavy mud ceiling. The water was now up to everyone's waists and there was a lot of sloshing and grunting as Mr. and Mrs. Bold coaxed a frightened Tony along as quickly as an arthritic, wet, scared hyena can go.

But after several tense minutes, tripping and sliding in the darkness, moonlight appeared at the end of the tunnel, and Mr. Bold ran ahead.

"We've made it!" he called back. "You can let go now, twins. But listen—scramble out of the way the second you can. There is no time to lose—we don't want that tunnel to collapse on top of you, whatever happens."

"I'll count to three, then we'll let go together and run for it," instructed a bedraggled Betty.

"OK," said Bobby, who could hardly speak his limbs hurt so much.

There came a deep groan from above them.

"One, two . . . three!" shouted Betty, and the twins dived towards the tunnel entrance, half running, half swimming through the ghastly thick sludge.

"Betty, Bobby!" called Mrs. Bold. "Hurry up!"

The ceiling collapsed behind them in an avalanche of splashing and crashing. They made it out in the nick of time—and as the twins fell, exhausted, against their parents, a final belch of filthy grey mud spat over everyone. They were safe and the tunnel was no more.

There was quiet for a moment. Then Bobby

and Betty began to giggle with relief.

"That was a narrow squeak!" said Mrs. Bold. "Look at you both! You're going to need a bath with bubbles."

"Who is Bubbles?" asked Mr. Bold. And everyone had a good laugh, which was just what was needed after such drama. But then Mr. Bold announced that they ought to get themselves back to Fairfield Road before anyone saw them—it wouldn't be long before the sun came up.

Mr. Bold got the old sack ready and called to a rather bewildered Tony.

"Here!" he said. "Jump in until we get you safely home." It was hard to tell in the gloom, but from poor Tony's groaning and muttering, he seemed to be safely in the sack.

Mrs. Bold and the twins then tidied up the entrance to the collapsed tunnel so it looked as if it had never been there, and Mr. Bold hoisted the heavy sack onto his shoulders and the grubby convoy made their way cautiously back to their car and set off home.

When Mr. Bold carried the sack containing Tony from the car into the house, a wide-eyed Mr. McNumpty looked on in horror. Who were these people? Burglars?

Once safely inside, Tony clambered out and sat on the sofa, looking nervously around.

"Would you like a drink of milk, dear?" asked Mrs. Bold. "You've been through quite an ordeal."

"Er, yes. I'll try one," said Tony, blinking and scratching at the mud on his tummy with his hind leg.

"Shall I get you a bucket of water?" asked Bobby helpfully. "Give you a bit of a wash down?"

"Thank you," said Tony.

Suddenly Betty let out a high-pitched scream. "The sack! It just moved!" she said, running to her father.

"Goodness, so it did," agreed Mr. Bold. "There's something in there."

"That will be Miranda," said Tony. "She's probably peckish. I don't suppose you have any grapes handy, do you?"

"Miranda?" said Mrs. Bold, astonished. "Who is Miranda?"

"Let me introduce you." Tony reached inside the sack and brought out a tiny, baby gray monkey with white fluffy ears, big black shiny eyes, and a long striped tail. She immediately jumped onto Tony's shoulder and peered at the Bolds nervously.

"This is Miranda, everyone," said Tony. "She's a marmoset monkey. An orphan."

"But what—" said Mr. Bold.

"The other monkeys rejected her, so she attached herself to me for some reason. When she heard I was leaving the safari park—all the animals knew about it, you see—she cried and cried until I said she could come with me. I'm sorry I didn't tell you before—I was worried in case you said no. Please let her stay. She'll be no bother."

"She's lovely!" said Betty, stroking Miranda gently. "Go on, Mum, let her stay. Pleeeeaaaase, Dad!"

"The more the merrier, I guess!" said Mr. Bold. And Mrs. Bold agreed.

"Thank you, thank you!" chorused Tony and Betty.

"The dear little girl! I'll cut up some grapes," said Mrs. Bold. "Does she speak?"

"Just baby talk at the moment," explained Tony. "But she's learning fast. She'll soon get used to you all."

What do you call a monkey with a banana in each ear?

Anything you like. She can't hear you!

After enjoying a nibble on some grapes, Miranda made a few contented squeaks and settled down for a rest against Tony.

"It's been quite a night!" said Mr. Bold. "Shall I show you to your room, Tony—and Miranda? I think it's time we all had a wash and some sleep!"

"Tell us another joke first, Dad," asked Bobby.

Mr. Bold laughed, then looked over at Miranda before saying,

Where do baby monkeys sleep?

Ape-ri-cots!

Chapter 12

There are two things you must teach a hyena if it comes to live with you in your suburban home: how to speak human and how to walk on its hind legs. Otherwise you will have all sorts of trouble with the neighbors.

The Bolds set to work the very next day: walking lessons for Tony in the morning, talking lessons after lunch.

There is a saying that "You can't teach an old dog new tricks," and although hyenas are very clever animals and Tony was keen to learn, that saying seemed to be true, unfortunately—

especially if the "dog," or should I say, "hyena," has arthritis. There was a lot of huffing and puffing, and poor Tony kept falling over backwards, knocking into things and making a terrible racket. But, despite all the noise and commotion, as they were hyenas they all had a good laugh about it.

And then Bobby had an idea. "Why don't you use a walking stick to keep your balance?"

he suggested, wiping tears of laughter from his eye. "Old people often have sticks to help them walk and keep them upright."

"Good thinking, Bobby," said Mr. Bold. "There's an old stick in the garden shed— go and get it, and we'll see if it helps."

But it didn't help much. Tony attempted tottering up and down the hallway with the stick, but he was still very unsteady. The problem was that for every three steps he took on his back legs he then did six on all fours. And there was no way that would ever pass as human behavior.

"These things take time," said Mrs. Bold patiently. But Tony seemed to be getting rather upset and wasn't laughing much any more.

Next the Bolds dressed him in a pair of tracksuit bottoms, a T-shirt, some slippers, and an old cloth cap—and he looked just like a rather hairy old man. Betty and Bobby roared with laughter when they saw him.

"Hot and itchy," was Tony's verdict.

Talking human was proving even more difficult than walking on two legs for Tony, and the afternoon's lessons were worse than the morning's.

Poor Tony's heart just wasn't in it. He couldn't see the point. "Can't I just pretend I'm foreign?" he sighed.

"Just learn the basics, Tony," pleaded Mr. Bold. "Like 'Hello,' 'Good-bye,' 'My name is Tony.' And you need to learn our address, in case you get lost."

"Hyenas don't get lost!" guffawed Tony. "We just sniff the air and smell our way back to where we came from. Or have you forgotten how to do that?" he added sarcastically.

"Suppose you have a cold?" asked Bobby. "Then what?"

"Well, if I have a cold I won't be going out in the first place, will I?" replied Tony.

"You won't want to be cooped up in the

house forever," said Mrs. Bold. "There's a big, wide world out there. Sooner or later you will want to go and investigate it. We want you to be free! There's Bushy Park, the library, the supermarket. Who knows? You might even want to go to London."

"Where?" said Tony.

Mrs. Bold sighed. "Maybe not."

"Let's face it," said Tony, shaking his head. "I'm never going to be able to walk or talk like humans. I'm an old hyena and that's that. Perhaps you should have left me in the safari park to die." Then he went—on all fours—up to his room and stayed there.

"Poor Tony," said Mr. Bold. "He's so unhappy. I feel terrible for him—and I haven't heard him laugh in days."

"Patience, dear," said Mrs. Bold. "It's still early days. We mustn't expect too much too soon."

Miranda the monkey, on the other hand, settled in very quickly. Her initial shyness soon went and she delighted in scampering up the curtains and swinging from the light fixtures, landing on the twins' heads when they least expected it, and making them shriek with laughter.

She could walk on her two back legs easily, and in her squeaky, high-pitched voice she was soon speaking semi-human—enough to be understood, and getting better every day.

And she was cheeky. She once filled her cheeks with water from the toilet, then opened the window and squirted it all over Mr. McNumpty as he was walking down his path.

Mr. McNumpty, who assumed he'd been fired at with a water pistol, shook his fist at the Bolds' house and called out, "Pests!"

Betty and Minnie took to dressing Miranda up in their dolls' clothes and pushing her up and down the garden path in the doll's carriage.

One day Bobby was watching them when he suddenly shouted: "*That's it! That's the answer!*"

"What are you jumping up and down about?" asked Minnie.

"The carriage. Don't you see? Bring it indoors and I'll show you. Where's Tony?"

Poor Tony had given up on learning things after a lesson on how to use the toilet had ended with disastrous results. He now spent most of his days curled up asleep on the kitchen floor, and because he couldn't leave the house he was bored and miserable. But there seemed to be nothing anyone could do to help him.

"Tony?" said Bobby gently, stroking the old hyena on the back. "Wake up, Tony. I've had an idea."

"Yes?" yawned Tony. "An idea, eh? Take me back to the safari park and let them put me to sleep?"

"No, silly," said Bobby. "We'd never do that. An idea to help you walk. Come and try."

By propping his front paws on the handlebars of the carriage, Tony found he could walk along easily on his hind legs, pushing the carriage in front of him as he went.

"I say!" said Tony triumphantly. "I can do it! I can walk like a human at last!"

"Faster, faster!" squeaked Miranda, who was still lying in the carriage, wearing a white lace gown with matching bonnet.

"I'll put my tracksuit on, then we can go in the garden," said Tony excitedly. Within

minutes he was expertly wheeling the little monkey in the carriage up and down the garden path.

"He looks so happy at last," said Mrs. Bold, watching from the patio. "Bravo, Tony!"

A few days later Tony felt confident enough to take Miranda in the carriage for a promenade along Fairfield Road, with the twins walking on either side of him just in case there was any unsteadiness. Tony was a bit alarmed by cars and bicycles—though he had seen many cars in the safari park—and he had to be taught how to cross the road safely.

"These black-and-white stripes are called a zebra crossing," explained Betty.

"Zebra? What zebra?" said Tony. "I can't smell a zebra. Don't have 'em in Teddington, do you?"

"No. Not a real zebra, silly," said Betty. "It's a place for people to cross the road, that's all."

"Look left, right, then left again," instructed Bobby. "And if there is nothing coming, cross over quickly."

"I see!" said Tony, once they were safely across. "It's easy when you know how."

By the next day Tony had decided he'd like to take the carriage out on his own.

"Are you sure you're ready, Tony?" asked a worried Mrs. Bold. "Will you be safe? What if someone speaks to you?"

"I've got Miranda with me. She'll answer for me."

So off they went. They made an odd-looking

couple, it's true: Miranda wrapped up in a pink gingham onesie and hood under a woolly blanket, and poor whiskery Tony stooped over the pram and hanging on for dear life, dressed in his saggy green tracksuit and cloth cap. But they managed a successful half-hour stroll all by themselves. Each day after that they went a little further, sometimes to the park where Miranda would play on the swings, and where Tony bought himself an ice cream by pointing and nodding.

At last the elderly hyena felt he was independent, able to leave the house and get some fresh air, and he was beginning to enjoy his new life. The rescue mission had been a success, and the Bolds' household was happy and full of laughter once more.

Mr. Bold loved having someone from the old country to chat to.

Mrs. Bold loved having someone around to watch the children so she could spend more time selling her hats.

And the children loved having Tony around to tell them stories, play games, and teach them the hyena war cry!

Chapter 13

But what of Mr. McNumpty? you're probably wondering. Well, his dislike of his neighbors was turning to angry bafflement. What on earth was going on in there? It was hard to keep up.

After that strange week of nighttime outings and mud-covered returns, things had seemed to return to normal—if anything was ever "normal" next door.

But then the noises started. Bumps and crashes, as if something or someone big and heavy was doing handstands against the wall . . . and there were strange high-pitched whistles and squeaks. A budgie? Two budgies? Sixteen? Mr. McNumpty didn't know, but he hardly slept for wondering about it all.

There was the water-squirting incident . . .

And on another occasion someone kept throwing grapes at him while he was hanging out his washing . . .

Unbeknown to the Bolds, Mr. McNumpty now spent most of his time spying on them. An old man seemed to be living with them now—an old man who dressed like a teenager and enjoyed wheeling a doll's carriage around? And what was that strange thing inside the carriage? A talking doll? A glove puppet? You couldn't make it up!

Mr. McNumpty used to watch television a

215

lot, but he didn't any more. There was a whole soap opera going on right next door that was far more interesting.

He had vowed not to speak to any of the Bolds ever again, which was a shame in a way because it prevented him from knocking on the door and having a jolly good argument with Mr. Bold, which he used to enjoy. Yet he was intrigued by the whole household and their peculiar behavior. Were they hippies? Mad people? Aliens from another planet? Or, as he'd always suspected . . . animals?

Sometimes he wished he had someone to moan about the Bolds to—someone who would understand how terribly annoying they were. But he didn't. There had never been a Mrs. McNumpty and there never would be. As for friends or relatives, there simply weren't any. Mr. McNumpty kept himself to himself.

Then one day, something terrible happened. Mr. McNumpty was on his way home from his usual weekly shop at the supermarket (six apples, three bananas, a chicken pie, two tins of sardines, a huge jar of honey, a loaf of bread, lamb chops, a nice bit of fish, some vegetables, a jumbo pack of toilet rolls, a bottle of dry sherry, and a bar of chocolate) when disaster struck. His sturdy shopping bag, which had served him well for many years (indeed, proclaimed itself to be "a bag for life!") suddenly gave way along its seams and fell apart.

Mr. McNumpty's precious purchases fell to the ground. Apples rolled into the gutter, tins under parked cars, bread, vegetables, chocolate, chops—everything sprawled across the pavement.

Mr. McNumpty stood **helplessly** rooted to the spot, unsure what to rescue first.

A gang of six or seven surly, bored youths with unnecessarily short haircuts who had been sitting on a wall smoking spotted him. They jeered at his distress, and then leaped off the wall and sauntered towards him, kicking his shopping items around as they laughed callously, delighted to have something to amuse themselves with.

"Clear off!" said Mr. McNumpty. "That's my shopping. I'll give you boys a good kicking if I catch you!"

But the Teddington Massive, as the youths were called, took no notice and, hoarse with laughter, took great delight in viciously squashing Mr. McNumpty's vegetables and stamping on his loaf of bread. They opened his sherry and began swigging it, passing it from one to another as they dodged the now-furious Mr. McNumpty who, red in the face and wheezing noisily, ran in circles trying to grab the agile youngsters.

"Help! Police!" cried Mr. McNumpty, running around aimlessly, still clutching his broken shopping bag. Finally he caught one boy who had paused to guzzle the sherry and gave him a hefty kick on the shin.

"Give that bottle back!" Mr. McNumpty demanded breathlessly.

"Oh yeah?" said the pimply boy, limping backwards.

He tossed the half-empty bottle to one of his friends, then lunged forward and pushed Mr. McNumpty to the ground. The atmosphere suddenly became very charged and serious. The youth's face was twisted with hatred, and danger hung in the air like mist.

"What now, old man?" the young thug spat.

Just then, as it so happened, Tony, who was having his daily outing with Miranda in the carriage, turned the corner of Fairfield Road and was confronted with the chaotic scene. Food was scattered all over the pavement and the angry mob was closing in on Mr. McNumpty, who was now frozen in fear.

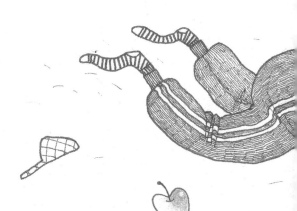

Animals have an instinctive reaction to evil, and without pausing to think of the consequences, Tony abandoned the carriage and with a hyena's blood-curdling war cry and an energy he hadn't displayed for many years, bounded on all fours towards the boys threatening Mr. McNumpty. "You brutes!" he roared (in animal language).

The gang scattered in terror, but Tony was too quick for them. His eyes glinting menacingly, drool hanging from his snarling jaws, he snapped at the sprinting ringleader, and sank his teeth into the boy's quivering rump.

There was a rip of cheap denim, the pimply youth howled in pain and fear and ran for his life, squawking like a parrot. Tony then turned his attention to the other boys, who scattered in all directions like sparks from a firework.

Drama over, Tony sat panting on the pavement for a few seconds. Then, noticing Mr. McNumpty staring at him with a mixture of disbelief and gratitude, he attempted to assume a more human-like demeanor. He cleared his throat, brushed himself down, then shuffled awkwardly back to the carriage and hoisted himself up again onto his back legs.

Miranda, meanwhile, had collected what was left of Mr. McNumpty's shopping and piled it into the now-empty carriage.

"No worry, Mr. McGrumpy," she said, in her squeaky voice. "We save your shopping!"

Mr. McNumpty stood in silence. He was in shock—so much had happened in the last two minutes he didn't know what he thought any more. One minute he had been walking home with his shopping, then a loathsome gang had attacked him, and now the people he had thought he hated had suddenly become his heroes.

But who or what was the old man? Could he really be . . . ? Much to his surprise, Mr. McNumpty's eyes filled with tears and he began to sob.

"I, I . . ." he tried to speak.

"Them nasty boys," interrupted Miranda as she climbed back into the carriage, perching on top of his battered shopping. "We get you home now. Nice cup of tea."

Chapter 14

Betty and Bobby could not believe their eyes when they looked out the front-room window and saw Miranda and Tony slowly walking a shaken Mr. McNumpty to his front door and then go inside with him. They looked at each other in shock.

"Did you just see what I saw?" asked Betty.

Bobby nodded. "I think so. Should we do something?"

"I don't know. Shall I call Mum in from the garden?"

"Probably." And the two of them rolled off the sofa, laughing.

Next door, Mr. McNumpty was in no fit state to be left alone. He slumped down on a chair while Tony put the kettle on and Miranda nimbly leaped from the carriage to the counter and back again, each time carrying an item of shopping.

"Thank you," the old man mumbled as Tony handed him a cup of tea. Tony nodded and patted Mr. McNumpty gently on the shoulder.

"He no speak English," explained Miranda. "He learn slow. Understand but no speak yet. Me speak for him."

"I see," said Mr. McNumpty weakly, taking a nice slurp of warm tea. "What country is he from?"

228

"Oh, er," said Miranda, "some place far, far away."

"He saved my life . . . I've been such a nasty, miserable fool . . . How can I ever thank him?"

"No need!" chirruped Miranda brightly. "Boys bad, Tony bite them good!" And she gave a flute-like hoot of laughter, and this set Tony off on a loud hyena cackle.

Mr. McNumpty's eyes widened in surprise. But the laughter was infectious, and before he knew it he was laughing himself. He hadn't laughed for years, and the feeling of it cheered him up instantly. "Those boys will think twice about stealing anybody's shopping in future!" he chuckled. "And that big one will have a good set of teeth marks on his backside. Sitting down is going to be a painful business for that young ruffian!"

They were all laughing loudly together now, and Tony's teeth were on full display.

"Blimey, you've got some teeth on you, Tony," said Mr. McNumpty admiringly. "I have to take mine out at night."

After the laughing stopped and the tea was finished, Miranda and Tony thought they should leave, but Mr. McNumpty seemed in no hurry to be on his own, so Miranda settled down in her carriage for a nap.

The two old boys sat thoughtfully at the table for a moment. Much to his surprise, Mr. McNumpty was enjoying the company of someone his own age. He'd never been one for a chat or a gossip, so the fact that Tony didn't speak didn't bother him in the slightest.

"Like a game of dominoes?" he asked.

Tony shrugged. "Romroes?" he tried to say.

"Dom-in-oes," said Mr. McNumpty slowly. "Don't suppose you know what dominoes is?"

Tony shook his head.

"Let me teach you, then. I've got a set somewhere . . ."

An hour later, when Miranda woke up from her snooze, the two new friends were hunched over the domino game, completely engrossed.

"Grapes, please, Mr. McNump?" yawned Miranda.

"No grapes, I'm afraid. Will an apple do?" asked Mr. McNumpty. He got one of the rescued apples from the counter and handed it to Miranda, who proceeded to nibble at it daintily. "And please," he said, blushing a little, "call me Nigel." He turned back to Tony and the dominoes. "My turn?"

Tony nodded.

A while later, the game was over and Tony and Miranda got ready to leave.

"Shall we play another game tomorrow?" asked Mr. McNumpty.

Tony nodded enthusiastically.

As they opened the front door, they found Mrs. Bold standing nervously on the doorstep with Betty and Bobby peeking out from behind her skirt. She had come rushing in from the garden when the twins called her and had been wondering ever since whether to go round to Mr. McNumpty's or not. Finally her curiosity and concern had gotten the better of her.

"Is everything all right?" she asked, but suddenly couldn't help giggling as she saw Mr. McNumpty put his hand affectionately on Tony's shoulder.

"Everything is fine. Absolutely fine. Miranda and Tony have been most kind, and we've just finished a delightful game of dominoes. Same time tomorrow, Tony?"

Tony nodded, and Betty and Bobby just couldn't help it—they broke out into the longest and loudest hyena laugh ever. Dominoes with Mr. McNumpty? Whatever next?

And so it was that Tony and Mr. McNumpty (or Nigel, as we are now allowed to call him) became firm, if unlikely, friends. A game of dominoes after Tony's afternoon walk became a daily tradition—and they even progressed to ice creams together at the ice-cream parlor, if you can imagine that.

It did Tony the world of good to have a friend, and he seemed much happier and more settled. And patiently, every day, Mr. McNumpty attempted to teach Tony a few more English words. Tony puckered his lips and bravely attempted to speak, but somehow his tongue seemed to get in the way and the words came out back to front.

"Never mind, at least you are trying," comforted Mr. McNumpty. "We'll get there one day."

Nigel's animosity towards his neighbors was replaced with smiles and—whenever he met Mrs. Bold—a gallant bow and a cheery "Hello!" He even put a Christmas card through their letterbox in early December, signed:

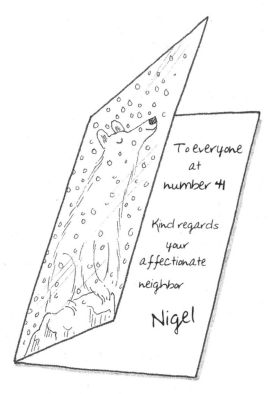

To everyone
at
number 41

Kind regards
your
affectionate
neighbor
Nigel

"Goodness, what a turnaround!" said Mr. Bold, placing the card on the mantelpiece.

"There was a nice man inside trying to get out all along," said Mrs. Bold. "It just took Tony to find him and winkle him out."

"Do you think we should invite him to Christmas dinner?" suggested Mr. Bold. "It seems a shame for him to be alone next door while we are all tucking into our turkey."

"Yes," said Mrs. Bold. "We've already got Minnie coming, as her parents are going to spend the day making soup for homeless people."

"Very kind of them," said Mr. Bold.

"Although it does mean we'll actually have to cook the turkey this year," pointed out Mrs. Bold, "which I doubt will be as tasty."

"It'll make a nice change," said Mr. Bold.

"And the two old fellows can have a nice game of dominoes after dinner."

"Perfect!" agreed Mrs. Bold, and she sighed contentedly.

Chapter 15

It had been several months since Tony's rescue from the safari park and now he and Miranda were well and truly a part of the Bold family.

One day Miranda, just like the twins, would make her own way in the world, but for now they were all happier than they had ever been.

The snow that year fell thick and fast all Christmas Eve, and the Bolds awoke to see a magical wonderland outside.

Father Christmas had not left their presents wrapped up under the tree as was usual, but instead had buried them in the garden, so before breakfast all the Bolds went outside in their pyjamas for a glorious dig. (Nigel McNumpty saw this from his window, of course, but he didn't mind what the Bolds did any more. In fact, he quite fancied having a dig himself . . .)

After much frantic excavation, all the presents were found. Tony had a pair of nice warm mittens, Miranda had a skipping rope, the twins had roller skates, and Mr. and Mrs. Bold shared a big glossy book about Africa, which included lots of photographs of places and animals they loved.

Christmas was Mr. Bold's **favorite** time of year. The Christmas tree glittered with fairy lights, the house was decked out with garlands

and holly and baubles, and the table was laid properly with napkins, candles and, of course, Christmas crackers. Because the best part of Christmas, in Mr. Bold's opinion, was that he could tell Christmas cracker jokes all day long.

Then a little later, Minnie and Nigel McNumpty arrived and they all sat round the kitchen table tucking into their lunch.

"Very tasty," said Nigel, rubbing his tummy. "Haven't had such a slap-up lunch in years!"

"Mum made you a cake once, but you slammed the door in her face," said Bobby.

"Now then," cautioned Mrs. Bold, "that's all in the past."

"No, you're right," said Nigel. "I behaved terribly, I know. I must say sorry."

"Apology accepted," said Mr. Bold, passing the box of chocolates to their guest. "Fancy another?"

Nigel popped a chocolate in his mouth.

"Mind you," said Mr. Bold, "I thought you were going to punch me in the nose over that incident with the bucket!"

"When was that?" asked Betty.

"You know," said Minnie helpfully. "Mr. McNumpty was up the ladder and dropped his bucket. It was the day I saw your tail and found out you were all hyenas." Then, realizing what she had said, she stopped and covered her mouth with her hand, but it was too late.

There was a terrible silence, and Minnie mouthed the word "Sorry" to Betty. No one knew what to say, and for once not a single hyena felt like laughing. They all stared at Nigel, and eventually he spoke.

"I know," he said simply. "Deep down I've always known. You are hyenas."

Mrs. Bold's mouth dropped open and everyone looked at Nigel in horrified surprise.

"But . . . you . . . how?" Mr. Bold tried his best to form a sentence.

"I met the original Fred and Amelia before they went on their honeymoon," Nigel explained. "I didn't actually speak to them. Didn't speak to anyone in those days. But then when they, or rather you, came back, I knew something wasn't right. Took me a while to work it out. Hyenas, eh?" He looked around the table. "Apart from you, Minnie, and Miranda."

"Monkey, monkey!" said Miranda.

"Yes. I figured as much."

"So why didn't you tell on us?" asked Bobby.

"You won't tell, will you?" asked Betty fearfully.

Nigel shook his head and looked at Betty kindly. "No, I shan't be telling anyone."

"But, I don't understand . . ." muttered Mrs. Bold. "I know you like us now. Since Tony saved you from that gang and you made friends—" she looked affectionately at Tony, who was following the conversation with rapt attention— "but before? Why didn't you tell anyone before?"

"You used to hate us!" said Bobby helpfully.

Nigel smiled. "I know, I know. But you see, we all have our secrets. And I was terrified you'd discover mine. That is why I was so nasty. I wanted to make sure you stayed away."

"Oh dear," said Mr. Bold. "This is all such a lot to take in. Can I tell another joke?"

"Not now, dear," said Mrs. Bold.

"So what's your secret, then?" asked Bobby.

"Well, I've never told anyone," said Nigel, wiping his forehead with his large hand.

"You know our secret," Bobby said encouragingly. "We're hyenas."

"Yes, you are. And very nice hyenas you are too. And more to the point, I trust you. All of you." He took a deep breath. "I am not really

Nigel McNumpty, the miserable old man from next door . . . In fact, I'm not a man at all. I am . . ." He paused, as if unable to say the words.

"Well?" asked Bobby.

"I'm an animal too. A grizzly bear."

There was a collective gasp from everyone.

"Grizzly bear?!" said Mr. Bold, impressed. "I didn't see that coming!"

(And neither did I, if I'm honest, and I don't suppose you did either—even the cleverest ones amongst you. This story just gets better and better!)

"How cool!" said Betty, taking a surreptitious look at Mr. McNumpty's surprisingly long nails.

What do you call a bear with no shoes on?

"Not now," said Mrs. Bold.

Bare foot!

"But how come?" asked Minnie, ignoring the joke. "Where are you from?"

"I was born in Alaska many, many years ago. I am indeed old. When I was born, I was truly wild and free, but when I was still a small cub my mother was killed by some fur hunters and I was taken into captivity."

"Oh no!" said Betty, a paw to her mouth. Miranda whimpered and ran onto Tony's lap.

"Shh!" said Mrs. Bold. "Let Nigel continue."

Mr. McNumpty smiled sadly, then carried on with his story. "From there I was bought and sold a few times until I struck lucky. I ended up as the prized pet of a rich, somewhat eccentric Arabian prince. I was more than a pet—I was his constant companion, his best friend. I learned how to speak in several languages and how to conduct myself in social circles. I wined and dined with heads of state, I played poker, I saw the best shows on Broadway, I dated some of the most beautiful women in the world—those were indeed very happy days."

He sighed wistfully at the memory.

"And when we weren't travelling around in first class, I lived in sumptuous style in the prince's palace. I wore a gold and diamond-encrusted collar and slept in a marble-floored den with my own servants on a four-poster bed under a Harrods' duvet."

"Wow! Imagine that!" said Betty.

"The prince and I were inseparable. We flew all over the world. Summer season in St. Tropez, skiing in Aspen, Hollywood parties, Ascot, the Oscars—"

"Red carpets!" Minnie squeaked, and Mr. McNumpty nodded at her.

"Yes, all right, we get the idea," interrupted Mr. Bold.

Why do bears wear fur coats?

Because we look silly in anoraks.

"Stop it with the jokes for just a minute, Dad," pleaded Bobby. "I want to know what happened next."

"Oops, pardon me," said Mr. Bold, trying to look serious, which was **impossible**.

"Yes, I want to know too," said Betty. "How come you ended up in a little house in Teddington?"

"Well," said Nigel, looking a little sad, "the prince simply got tired of me. Got a new plaything. A leggy brunette. Ostrich, I think she was. A flighty thing, but very seductive eyes. I was surplus to requirements."

"So why didn't he just send you back to Alaska?" asked Minnie reasonably.

"I knew too much," answered Nigel, lowering his voice. "All of his secrets . . . and to answer your question about how I ended up here, I really don't know the answer. One minute I was eating smoked salmon by the pool at the Hotel du Paris in Monte Carlo, and the next thing I knew I woke up here, feeling decidedly woozy. And alone. I thought that the salmon tasted odd . . . I think I must have been drugged.

"Here I found a wardrobe full of cheap clothing in my size and details of a bank account in my name . . . I receive a monthly allowance from the prince—he is a generous man. So this became my life. I've tried to keep myself to myself ever since—a question of survival."

"Gosh," said Mrs. Bold after a respectful silence. "That's quite a story. No wonder you were miserable!"

"But I think—I hope," said Nigel, "that we can put all of that behind us. The past is done with. What matters is that we are all here, living happily next door to each other. How we got here isn't important, surely?"

"You're quite right," agreed Mrs. Bold, reaching for the cheeseboard.

"May I, now?" asked Mr. Bold, who had been fidgeting throughout Mr. McNumpty's story. "It is Christmas Day, after all!"

"Yes, dear, you may now tell us all a joke," said Mrs. Bold.

Why are bears large, brown, and hairy?

"Because," answered Mr. McNumpty with a sigh,

If we were small, white, and smooth we'd be eggs!

"You seem to have heard all the bear jokes before," said Mr. Bold, somewhat crestfallen.

"Oh yes. Heard 'em all many times," confirmed Mr. McNumpty. "When I was with the prince."

Just then there was a loud crack and everyone turned to look at Tony, who had a look of astonishment on his face. He was holding in each paw the two ends of a Christmas cracker.

"Don't worry, Tony," said Betty, who was sitting next to him. "They're meant to make that noise. It's all part of the fun!" And she gave poor Tony a reassuring scratch behind his ears.

Mr. Bold picked up the small folded piece of paper that had fallen onto Tony's plate as Tony sniffed one half of the cracker tentatively for a moment, and then swallowed it in one gulp.

What do you get when you eat a Christmas cracker?

read Fred. Everyone thought for a moment.

Tinsel-itis?

answered Tony, bits of chewed-up gold paper falling from his mouth.

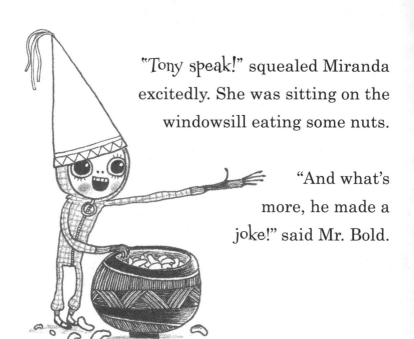

"Tony speak!" squealed Miranda excitedly. She was sitting on the windowsill eating some nuts.

"And what's more, he made a joke!" said Mr. Bold.

"Hurrah! Merry Christmas to all hyenas everywhere!"

Everyone cheered and laughed until they thought they would burst, and beneath his furry cheeks Tony blushed with pride.

"Merry Christmas!" he said loudly. "Happy Christmas, everyone!"

And that is where we shall leave them— pulling crackers, telling jokes, and laughing.

I told you at the beginning that this would be a funny peculiar story, didn't I? Well, I hope you've enjoyed it. Now all you need to remember is that it's true—every word.

I NEVER tell lies.

When **Julian Clary** isn't having a silly time dressing up and telling jokes on stage, he loves to be at home with his pets. He has lots of them: dogs, cats, ducks, and chickens. His lifelong love of animals inspired him to tell a story about what would happen if they pretended to be like us. Julian can't wait to read his books aloud to children and animals around the country.

David Roberts always loved to draw and paint as a child, and when he grew up his talents took him all the way to Hong Kong where he got a job making beautiful hats. But he always wanted to illustrate children's books, and so he came back to England to work with the finest authors in the land. David loves drawing animals and clothes and hats, so what could be better than a book about animals *in* clothes and hats?

Praise for THE BOLDS

"In its quirky, unique way, this explores themes of family and what constitutes human nature. . . . This entertaining tale will make readers chortle. A good choice for reluctant readers and fans of Captain Underpants."
—*Booklist Online*

★ "The book's hilarious plot and abundant illustrations make it a top choice for reluctant readers. . . . Wildly original and very funny." —starred, *Kirkus Reviews*

"Clary mixes animal fact with imaginative, entertaining fiction." —*Publishers Weekly*

"Fans of Roald Dahl will find much to appreciate here."
—*School Library Journal*

★ "Middle-graders will revel in the low-brow silliness, with delightful illustrations of the joyful, sharp-toothed hyena family. . . . A celebration of ingenuity, tolerance, untiring good humor and big hyena hearts."
—starred, *Shelf Awareness*

More adventures await THE BOLDS
and their friends in The Bolds to the Rescue

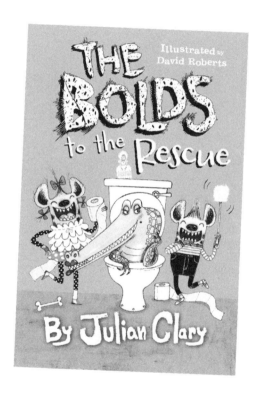

Chapter

A word of warning before I start: it's probably best to keep this book away from grown-ups. They just won't understand it. They'll say it's "a load of silly nonsense!" or ask, "Why don't you read something more sensible?"

Well, grown-ups aren't always right. (I'm a grown-up myself, so I should know.) They read boring newspapers and tedious, thick books with no pictures and no jokes in them where nothing interesting happens, ever.

So much happens in THIS book, I'm not even sure where to begin. It is a very unusual book. As you are about to find out. But unusual doesn't mean it is silly or a load of nonsense. It is a true story. Make no mistake about it. You will understand that. Grown-ups won't.

And if a grown-up happens to be reading this to you as a bedtime story, then they must keep their remarks to themself.

There, then. I've gotten that off my chest, so let's begin.

Have you ever heard of the Bolds? You probably have. They're a lovely family who live at 41 Fairfield Road in Teddington. They're always laughing, always joking. Mr. Bold works in the local Christmas cracker factory, writing the jokes. Mrs. Bold makes and sells elaborate hats at

the local market. And their twins, Betty and Bobby, are such sweet, adorable children.

Also living with them are Uncle Tony and Miranda, who they rescued from a safari park. Yes, that's right, a safari park—you did hear me correctly. Because the Bolds are a rather unusual family who do unusual things. We all have secrets, but their secret is BIGGER and hairier than most . . .

You see, behind closed doors they're not a family like yours or mine. A human family. Oh dear me, no. They're a family of hyenas pretending to be humans—from the tips of their furry ears right down to their paws.

No one knows. Except us.

You're probably in shock. Indeed, so was I when I first heard about them, but in actual fact it's **not** as shocking as you might think. There are a **lot** of animals out there living their lives pretending to be humans. **Giraffes** who stack shelves in grocery stores, **pigs** who eat popcorn noisily all the way through films in the cinema, **bulldogs** who work outside nightclubs. In fact, the Bolds' next-door neighbor, Mr. McNumpty, is an animal too. A **grizzly bear**.

And while he and the Bolds have had their differences in the past, he's now firm friends with them and pops over most evenings for a game of dominoes and a couple of pork chops.

Except for Tuesdays. There are no games of dominoes that night because Tuesday nights in the Bolds' neat semi-detached house are very special. Tuesday nights are Grooming Night. You might think this means face masks and manicures, but you'd be wrong. In fact the Bolds, and deaf old Uncle Tony, and Miranda the marmoset monkey, all sit in a circle, scratching, rubbing, and nibbling each other, making sure all the loose fur comes out and any bits of mud or fluff that might be lurking there are removed. Not to mention the fleas . . .

Obviously they have to make sure the curtains are drawn and no one peeps in. Although we humans sometimes scratch and itch too, we aren't often seen lying on our backs while our mothers **nibble** at our tummies with sharp teeth, or found **licking** each other's ears with big, long tongues that reach right across our faces to the other ear and beyond.

Enjoyable and good for the Bolds as this is, the activity tickles too, so everyone at Number 41 ends up **giggling** and **whooping** with laughter. This just gets them in the mood to listen to some of Mr. Bold's latest jokes:

Why did the banana go to the doctor?

Because he wasn't peeling well!

Or:

Why did the jelly wobble?

Because it saw
the milk shake!

And before long, on Tuesday nights in 41 Fairfield Road, everyone is **rolling** on the floor in laughter.

Now, one Tuesday evening, once the grooming was done and the twins had gone to bed, Mrs. Bold went to the bathroom to brush her teeth and wash and moisturize her friendly, furry face. The moment she sat on the toilet seat, she thought she heard a faint cough followed by a splashing sound. She cocked her ear to one side and listened intently. Hyenas have very good hearing.

Then she blinked in confusion as she realized the sounds she was hearing were coming from beneath her . . . from inside the toilet bowl!

But before she could jump up to take a look she felt a little nip on her bottom.

"Shrieeek!" she cried and shot up into the air. She then peered cautiously into the toilet.

A head with two huge green eyes and a very long snout peered up at her and said in a deep, gravelly voice: "So sorry! It's only little me!"

Whatever this creature was, he or she seemed to have a LOT of teeth . . .

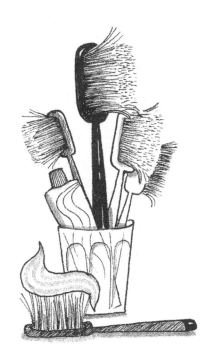